WHITE WOLF'S PACK

Hal Dunning

GUNSMOKE

First published in the UK by Isis

This hardback edition 2012
by AudioGO Ltd
by arrangement with
Golden West Literary Agency

ISBN 978 1 445 82409 3

British Library Cataloguing in Publication Data available.

Printed and bound in Great Britain by the MPG Books Group

Harold 'Hal' C. **Dunning** came from Westport, Connecticut, resided there most of his life, and is buried in the Dunning family plot in the Episcopal Cemetery in Cedarhurst. He was a short story writer for Street & Smith magazines for most of his life. Like Clarence E. Mulford, who created Hopalong Cassidy, Dunning wrote Western fiction while living primarily in the eastern United States. Unlike Mulford who maintained a permanent residence, Dunning was a creature of hotel rooms—even after he married—and eschewed permanent residence anywhere, living in a hotel in Quebec, Canada, with his family in Westport, and hotels in Flushing, New York; Newport, Rhode Island; Provincetown, Massachusetts, and in Westport. He was visiting a friend in Greenwich Village, New York when he died of a heart attack on July 29, 1931. What supported this itinerant lifestyle was the tremendous popularity of his character known as the White Wolf, outlaw Jim-twin Allen whose eyes were flecked with yellow and wolf-slanted. He rode alone with his two gray cow ponies, Princess and Gray Combat. The one man Jim-twin Allen could trust was his brother, Sheriff Jack-twin Allen, and often the little, freckle-faced gunman would come to his aid. The White Wolf stories were showcased in Street & Smith's *Complete Stories*, a bi-weekly supported largely by Hal Dunning's stories. Several of these stories were welded together to form books, all, published by Chelsea House: *The Outlaw Sheriff* (1928), *White Wolf's Law* (1928), *White Wolf's Pack* (1929), *The Wolf Deputy* (1930), *White Wolf's Feud* (1930), and the posthumous *White Wolf's Outlaw Legion* (1933). When Dunning died so unexpectedly, Street & Smith was faced with a financial crisis since *Complete Stories* could not survive without Jim-twin Allen. Author Frederick C. Davis was hired to continue the stories under the Hal Dunning byline, while Mrs. Cecily Dunning, the author's widow, was paid $60 every time her husband's name was used. Toward the end of the decade the Jim-twin Allen stories were continued by Walker A. Tompkins writing as Hal Dunning in Street & Smith's *Wild West Weekly*.

CHAPTER
ONE

Jim Allen's Promise

On the edge of the verandah sat "Toothpick" Jarrick. His weather-beaten countenance wore an expression of bewildered dismay. He had ridden more than a hundred miles to see an old friend and had found the friend so changed that he hardly knew him. Duff Dorwin leaned back in his chair, hooked his spurred heels over the railing, and grinned at Toothpick.

"You sure look like a calf what has lost its ma," he commented. Toothpick looked at Dorwin with perplexed eyes.

"As to that, I ain't sayin' you're wrong," he answered. "I can't say I'm sorry he's changed. Maybe it's better for him. But it's sure like meetin' a stranger. He's more like a lamb than a wolf."

He flung out a hand toward a small man in tattered jeans who was saddling a horse at the corral some hundred yards from the house.

"Look at the little runt. He always did look like a damn kid, but since he's laid away them guns of hisn, he don't look old enough to be livin' out in this damn lonesome place by hisself."

Toothpick lapsed into a moody silence. Duff Dorwin squinted at the tattered figure by the corral for a moment, then he grinned again.

"If I didn't know you I'd say you was the damnedest liar west of the Mississippi when you tole me that runt was 'Jim-twin' Allen what they called the 'Wolf,'" he said.

"Well, he is — only he ain't."

Dorwin looked at the lanky cow-puncher for an instant, then he looked away again.

"An' you think he ain't lyin' when he says he never packs a gun no more?" he asked at last.

"I'm bettin' a million on it. There's one thing even his worst enemy never said about Jim Allen. No one ever said he was a liar."

"You'd bet a million? But if he's as fast and sure as folks says, the gent what pulled on him would be bettin' his life if the Wolf was foolin'," Dorwin said slowly.

Something in the way he drawled out the words made Toothpick swing about and stare sharply at him.

"You wasn't aimin' to collect that reward on him, was you?" Toothpick cried hotly. "'Cause I'm tellin' you flat if you tried that an' he didn't draw on you, I sure would."

Duff Dorwin's pale-blue eyes met Toothpick's angry ones for an instant without flinching, then he shrugged and shook his head.

"Don't be goin' off the handle," he said soothingly. "Shucks, I knows that Allen is safe in this state, that he got a full pardon for savin' the governor's kid. Anyway, you know I'm square or you wouldn't have asked me to come over with you to get him to help us clean up them 'Black Hawks.' So pull your horns in and don't be glarin' at me that a way. I never did see a redhead that wasn't a menace to the community."

Toothpick relaxed and grinned sheepishly.

"Sure, I knows you're square, an' I reckon I'm sort o' hotheaded when folks talks about him, 'cause four or five times if it hadn't been for him, I'd been eatin' daisies by the roots."

"Why for did you go scaddlin' along back trails when you asked him to come and help clean out the Black Hawks? Why not come out blunt and plain?" Dorwin asked lazily.

"'Cause why? 'Cause Jim there's been ridin' the long trail for close to a dozen years, ever since he was a kid of eighteen, and outlaws is his friends. Hell! The law is chasin' him, an' you want me to ask him plain to help us nab some other gents what is dodgin' the law."

"I don't savvy all that," Dorwin argued. "Jim Allen has cleaned up some of the worst outlaws in this country."

"That's different. He done that 'cause they started to mix it personal with him. No, sir, Jim won't tangle with no gent what plays the game while rustlin' or playin' road agent."

"Why for did we come huntin' for him, then?"

"'Cause I was sort o' hopin' if he'd come visit 'Old Lady' Reiker — who's a grand old lady no matter what kind of skinflint that brother of hers, Bill Reiker, is — he'd stay a while, an' maybe them Black Hawks would start somethin' while he was there and make it personal with him. Then he'd wipe 'em out, an' she'd stop worryin'." Toothpick paused and mumbled: "An' I ain't give up all hope yet."

"Ain't you scared the lamb might turn wolf again when he learned you foxed him?"

"Not any. Not after he sees Old Lady Reiker an' eats her pies."

"If he don't pack no guns, what good would he be? Maybe you figure he'd start packin' 'em again," Duff persisted.

Toothpick shook his head regretfully.

"No, I figure Jim has packed a gun for the last time. When he sent them guns of hisn to 'Snippets' an' tole her he was through, he sure meant it, and he'll stick by it. But he don't need to do no killin' an' break his word, 'cause he could smell them coyotes out an' let us do the killin'."

Duff looked thoughtfully at Allen, who was now walking toward them, followed by three horses. Then he frowned and stroked his narrow chin.

"Huh, I sure hope you get him to come, then. It would mean sure I'd be sheriff again for another term if them Black Hawks is busted up," he said.

"It sure would," Toothpick agreed.

Both watched Allen's approach for a minute, then Duff Dorwin spoke suddenly:

"Toothpick, you ain't still suspicionin' me, are you, like you did a while ago?"

The tall cow-puncher stared at him in surprise.

"Hell, no! Why for you still thinkin' of that? I knows you're straight, or I sure would talk war talk now."

Jim-twin Allen's face split in a broad, loose grin as he greeted the two on the porch. He was a small, slender man of close to thirty, but he seemed no more than twenty. Big freckles covered his pug nose, and his curious eyes slanted at the corners like those of an animal. His nondescript garments were clean, but patched and worn. He pointed to the three grey horses. All were mares. Two of them were tall and gaunt with small, wicked heads; but the third, while she resembled the others, was less angular and more graceful.

"Hey, Toothpick, you know Princess. That there one what looks more like a goat even than her is Queen Second. The other is also Princess' daughter, but ain't she a beaut comin' from such an ugly old nag?" Allen cried boyishly.

"She sure is!" admired Toothpick.

"What you keepin' the other two for? Goin' to use 'em for crow bait?" Duff Dorwin asked with a laugh.

Allen's face clouded; he cast a quick glance at Duff. Then he ignored him and turned to the old mare.

"Duff, you ain't done nothin' but make breaks to-day," Toothpick said. "If you warn't all fat under your hat, you'd sure savvy if them hosses ain't beauties they got lines what tells of somethin' better — speed and bottom."

He knew how Allen felt toward these horses that had been his only companions for months at a time along the lonely trail, so he carefully phrased his reproof to Duff in a bantering manner. Toothpick still had hopes of persuading Allen to come and help them to ferret out the Black Hawks. It would not do to have Dorwin and Allen antagonistic.

"Shucks, I was only funnin'. Ain't I heard about them hosses what can run for ever an' then run some more?" Dorwin said, with a chuckle.

Allen's face cleared, but Toothpick looked curiously at Duff. Maybe the man had been joking, yet it was not what he had said, but his tone that was puzzling. Had Duff spoken deliberately to test something? Toothpick was still weighing this in his mind when Allen announced that he intended to ride a part of the way with them on their return journey.

"I'll travel along with you as far as the Whisperin' Hills, then come back here to-morrow," he said.

"Why don't you keep comin' with me to Old Lady Reiker's an' make me bust right out with tears of joy?" Toothpick cried eagerly. He told himself that if Allen went halfway he had won.

But Allen shook his head. The three saddled their horses. Allen rode Princess, put a pack on Queen Second; and she and the third grey followed them as they swung away from the ranch on the trail toward the Whispering Hills. Once Allen turned and looked back at his small abode. It consisted of a three-room house, a barn and a fenced meadow in a narrow valley surrounded by wild and broken country.

"She ain't much, but what there is of her is right pretty," he said.

"She sure is. How many head you got?" Toothpick asked.

8

"Thirty-seven. I don't keep nothin' but greys. Honey Boy is head of my string."

"It's a darned lonely place. I bet you don't see no one oftener than once a month," said Duff.

"I'm sort o' used to bein' alone, an' she's the first home I've had since I was a kid," Allen answered soberly.

That evening they camped in the foothills of the Whispering Hills country. Duff Dorwin announced that he would push on for Beaverville directly after supper. He had re-saddled his horse and was ready to leave when he turned suddenly to Allen.

"Jim, I bet you drinks for the house that Toothpick wins and I see you in Beaverville to-morrow," he said. Then he added, as if carried away by enthusiasm: "An' that means the end of the Black Hawks."

Without waiting for a reply, he waved his hand and trotted off into the darkness. The two stood in silence until the sound of his horse's hoofs died away; then Allen glanced at Toothpick's flushed and angry face.

"What you goin' to win an' who are the Black Hawks?" he asked.

"The cross-eyed Siwash! I never knowed he was so damned dumb!" The tall cow-puncher's voice trailed into silence — an admission of the futility of trying to find words to express his wrath.

Allen chuckled.

"Huh, so you was tryin' to put somethin' over on me, an' he spilled the beans?"

9

Toothpick opened his mouth, changed his mind, and closed it again.

"Is Old Lady Reiker what makes them wonderful apple pies, what you was coaxin' me to come an' guzzle, bein' raided by these Black Hawks?" Allen persisted.

"Yes. Her and every other person in the valley don't dare sleep at night 'cause of them skunks," Toothpick admitted.

"An' you figured if you got me there eatin' pies, I'd start tanglin' with them Black Hawks?"

"Yeah," Toothpick said shamefacedly. "Sure, Jim, I was tryin' to trick you. But Old Lady Reiker is a wonderful lady. She sure needs help bad. I knew you wouldn't come help if I asked you right out, but I figgered if you got to like the old lady you'd do something. I told that idjiot, Duff, about my scheme. Why for does he have to shoot off his mouth? Now, of course, you won't come."

"Who are these Black Hawks?"

"They're a secret society what goes around in black masks and gowns. They was started about a year ago as a sort o' vigilance committee. Every gent what was decent was a member then, 'cause the sheriff was no good, an' they was workin' hard for law an' order. Since the mines opened at Land's End, the valley has filled with tinhorns an' bad ones. It got so a woman didn't dare go out alone, an' the sheriff wouldn't do nothin', so they formed the Black Hawks and cleaned up. Then the job bein' done, the decent folks dropped out, an' a lot of wrong ones joined. Now things is worse than they

10

ever was. Folks is scared to speak above their breaths. The damned Black Hawks run everything. They string gents up. They whip 'em, an' they even whip women, burn barns, rustle cattle — an' folks don't dare object."

"Duff Dorwin, this sheriff — was he a member once?"

"Yes, but he quit when he was elected sheriff."

"What kind of gent is he?"

"He's not very fast with a gun, but he's a nervy cuss, an' folks like him 'cause he's square an' tryin' hard to clean up the Black Hawks. Some folks says he smiles a lot with his mouth but not with his eyes, an' he talks a lot but don't never tell you nothin'. Darn him, when he spilled the beans to you, it was the first time I ever knowed him to be so dumb."

"He don't look dumb," Allen said dryly. He was silent for a long time. When he spoke at last, his words came slowly, as though they hurt.

"Snippets is sure-enough goin' to get hitched?"

"Folks all say so," Toothpick replied gruffly. He would have given his right arm could he have answered otherwise, for he knew what Snippets MacPherson meant to Allen.

"Wouldn't do no harm if I see her then an' give her that grey," Allen said wistfully.

"That good-lookin' grey colt?"

"Yeah. I been trainin' that colt special for her ever since I see her two years ago, an' I'd sort o' like to show Snippets how the colt does her tricks." Allen's voice was boyishly eager, despite its wistful sadness.

Toothpick was silent in sympathy for a time. Then, little by little, the full significance of Allen's words came to him.

"Meanin' you're comin' to Beaverville?" he cried.

"I'll give Snippets her horse an' eat some of those pies, but I ain't promisin' anything else, 'cause, Toothpick, I ain't never wearin' my guns no more," said Allen firmly.

CHAPTER
TWO

White Wolf Returns

Beaverville had once aspired to be a metropolis, had boasted several real-estate offices and a couple of thousand inhabitants; but when the railroad decided to use Bender's Pass rather than Land's End, the realtors closed their offices, and the population shrank rapidly to a scant five hundred. Most of those who remained were of the unsavoury type of range hobo, hangers-on about the saloons, and tinhorn gamblers. The whole of Pleasant Valley became a nest of bandits, and killings became so common that the place earned the ugly sobriquet of Murder Valley. Two years before, Jim Allen, aided by several ranchers, had cleaned out the place; but since the mines had opened at Land's End, the town had reverted slowly to type. Once more it was the hangout of gangs of desperate men.

At the bar of the Lone Star Hotel, two cow-punchers were arguing with Mike, the fat bartender. Mike wiped his gleaming bald head and his red face with a soiled bandanna.

"Nope, you boys has had enough," he announced. Then he lowered his voice so that it would not reach two men at the farther end of the bar. "Besides which, you is talkin' too damn loud."

"Meanin' to say you figger the Bar II Bar boys should sew up their mouths just 'cause these here Black Hawks has ears?" Nat Price, the taller of the two, asked aggressively.

"All Black Hawks is yellow coyotes, and we boys has dirt behind our ears!" shouted "Shorty," the other puncher, pounding the bar.

Mike shrugged resignedly. He gave a quick glance at the two at the other end of the bar; then he slid out a bottle and glasses for the punchers. He realized that they had reached the stage of drunkenness where his greatest act of kindness to them would be to make them pass out. So he left them to themselves with the bottle. At a nod from the other two men, he produced another bottle and placed it before them. His manner to these two was in marked contrast to the way he had treated the two punchers. There was no familiarity here; he was watchful but not deferential.

Both of the men were of medium height and rather slender in build; both wore two guns tied down at their hips. "Kid" Moore had light hair and blue eyes. "Curly" Cole was dark skinned and black eyed, with tightly curled black hair. But despite the difference of their complexions, their expressions were the same: cold, hard, with straight mouths and eyes like marble.

To Mike's relief, they ignored the loud drunken talk of the two cow-punchers who were now outdoing each other in their threats against the Black Hawks. It was rumoured that both of these gunmen were members of that secret society. Hence Mike's fear for the cow-punchers. He sighed with relief when the gunmen walked to the door and passed into the street with never a look at the punchers.

"Gosh, you two old tumblebugs is sure fools for luck," he breathed fervently.

"You think we-all is scared of that there Kid Moore and Curly Cole!" Nat Price roared with laughter.

"We is lightnin' with guns." To prove his words Shorty sent a fumbling hand towards his holster and yanked at his gun. He succeeded in spilling it on the floor.

Mike was about to curse them both for fools when the swinging doors opened, and Toothpick clattered up to the bar, followed by a grinning, freckle-faced boy. Mike's mouth opened wide in astonishment; a light gleamed in his eyes, and he smiled a welcome.

"Hello, Toothpick. Hello, Ji —" He broke off and ended feebly: "'Lo, stranger."

"'Lo, Mike." Allen thrust his hand across the bar to shake the bartender's big, hairy paw.

Mike cast a quick glance about; he saw that the two punchers were too maudlin to understand even if they heard him.

"You comin' back to clean the valley again?" he asked eagerly. Allen shook his head.

"'Cause if you is, you come to me. A barkeep picks up bits of things, an' if he puts them together straight, they mean a lot," Mike continued. Then he frowned suddenly and stared at Allen as though he missed

15

something. "Your guns!" he exclaimed in dismay. "Then it's gospel you ain't packin' 'em no more."

"I reckon you heard correct, Mike. I ain't never goin' to pack no guns no more ever."

"But, Jim, Kid Moore is here in town, an' he's a bad one." When Allen's face expressed no alarm at that news, Mike went on. "The Kid is 'Stinger' Moore's brother. Hell, Jim, you recollect Stinger Moore. You dropped him that day with Jack Hart and 'Black Dick' — the day you rid your hoss to death to save 'Mac' MacPherson."

Allen's face clouded for a moment at the remembrance of Queen, his pet grey. Then he nodded and grinned.

"Sure, I remembers. Hell, Mike, my throat is plumb raw swallowin' alkali dust, an' you stand there gabbin'," he reproached.

"Did you get me when I said Kid Moore, Stinger's brother, just left here?"

"Sure he got you! Rustle that beer, Mike, an' we'll be hittin' it out of town!" Toothpick cried hurriedly. Mike's news seemed to disturb him far more than it did Allen.

As Mike fumbled beneath the bar for two bottles of beer he thought things over to himself. Allen claimed he was unarmed, but no unarmed man would have received the news that a killer, with whom he had a blood feud, was in town, as calmly as had Allen. Kid Moore would kill him on sight if he were really unarmed. Allen must have a gun secreted about him

16

somewhere. That was why he was unafraid. Mike grinned.

But Toothpick knew that Allen had spoken the truth, that he was really unarmed. Therefore he downed his beer with a gulp and fidgeted when Mike drew Allen to one side and began to whisper. Allen kept shaking his head; finally Mike stopped whispering and looked in abject dismay at Toothpick, who was nervously looking from the door to Allen.

Suddenly both Toothpick and Mike stiffened. The door swayed and opened; Curly Cole sauntered up to the bar. Both men stood rigid and waited for Kid Moore to follow. But when seconds passed and the other killer did not appear, their pent-up breath escaped in rushing sighs.

Curly Cole glanced at Allen from the corners of his eyes. At first something like fear flickered across his hard face; then this gave way to doubt. Finally his brow puckered, and he turned and stared frankly at Allen, looking him up and down from his shabby moccasins to his floppy black hat.

Then he said: "'Lo, kid, have a drink. You sure gave me a start. I thought you was —"

Allen interrupted quietly: "Jim Allen. That's me."

For a moment astonishment held Curly speechless. He had heard the rumour that the Wolf had forsaken his guns, but, like most people, had given little credence to it. Now he saw that Allen certainly carried no weapons in view. But was that bulge in his torn waistcoat, under his left arm, made by a sack of tobacco or by a gun?

"I hears tell you ain't packin' guns no more." Curly's voice held a perceptible sneer.

"Let me tell you —" began Toothpick, stepping forward, but Allen waved him aside.

"Keep out of this," he commanded. Then he added softly to Curly: "An' if I ain't, what then?"

Curly remained silent for a moment; he was trying to think out this puzzle. But Allen's eyes caught and held his; it was difficult to adjust his thoughts when faced with those strange eyes through which danced flecks of yellow fire. If Allen was unarmed and he, Curly, killed him now, no jury in the world would hold him for it. He could claim, and they would believe him, that Allen was armed. A lion might as well pretend he was a lamb as the Wolf pretend to be without his teeth. All he had to do was to draw and shoot; his name as a gunman would sweep up and down the border. He discounted Toothpick entirely; he could drop him with his left-hand gun.

But if Allen was really armed! That was the rub. If he did have a gun in a shoulder holster, then the chances were that Curly would not be known as a famous gunman, but only as a common corpse.

"Well, Mr. Wolf, I'm tellin' you somethin'. Kid Moore's in town, an' he's sure hankerin' to talk through smoke with you, 'cause of Stinger, his brother. He figgers you didn't down him fair." Curly's voice combined bluster and a sneer as he parried for time to make his decision.

"Maybe it warn't fair, but as I remembers it, Stinger had a couple of friends with him. Maybe you heard tell

18

of them — Bill Hart an' Black — an' I sure counted afore I went for my guns." Allen's voice went suddenly flat. "You tell Kid Moore that I don't pack no guns, an' in spite of that I ain't runnin' away."

Again those yellow eyes bored at Curly; the gunman was cowed.

"Well, I warned you fair," he sneered, then he swung on his heel and clumped out of the saloon. Better lose fame than take a chance on Jim-twin Allen.

"Gosh, you bluffed that black killer, an' you didn't have no gun!" gasped Mike.

"Jim, let's get out of here," Toothpick cried. He fairly pushed Allen from the saloon. When they were mounted at last and trotting out of town, followed by the two loose greys, the lanky cow-puncher gave a sigh of relief.

"Jim, you got to pack a gun; you can't go runnin' blazers all the time like that," he said earnestly.

"Just the same, I'll never pack another gun."

Toothpick looked at his friend; the freckled face was set firmly.

They rode on in silence. A few miles from Beaverville the trail climbed and turned sharply to the left toward the Bad Lands, a stretch of arid ground with stunted brush. Farther along, it skirted Black Butte and headed back toward Muddy Creek.

At the point where the trail flattened, they met a wagon drawn by two spindle-legged horses. It was driven by a middle-aged man and piled high with a miscellaneous collection of furniture. A woman and two small children sat beside the man.

19

"Hello, Biddle. Howdy, Missis Biddle. You movin'?" Toothpick greeted.

The man pulled his tired horses to a standstill and gave a hopeless little gesture.

"Yeah, we're leavin'," he mumbled.

"How come? You had a right nice place."

Toothpick knew the answer. The patches of tar on the man's arms and neck told him that, but he hoped to have Biddle tell his own story for Allen's benefit.

"Now, Bid, don't be talkin'," the woman pleaded fearfully.

"Yeah, I had a nice place. But I was told to go, so I'm goin'." The man's hands clenched in helpless anger.

"Black Hawks?"

At the mention of that name, the two children began to whimper, and the woman glanced about fearfully. Biddle scowled, picked up the reins, nodded to Toothpick, and the wagon went screeching on its way.

"You saw it?" asked Toothpick.

"Yeah, the Black Hawks tarred and feathered him. Why for did they do it?"

"How do I know? For nothin' a-tall, most probably."

Allen swung about and galloped back until he overtook the wagon. He wasted no preliminaries.

"Mister, I don't know you, an' you don't know me, but I'm Jim Allen. I ain't askin' you to talk now. But if you want to write to Mike at the Lone Star an' tell him why you're leavin' the valley, it won't do no harm, 'cause you'll be safe an' far away."

With that, he swung about and rejoined Toothpick.

"Why the hell don't some of you gents get together and clean out these here Black Hawks?" he demanded.

"Ain't there several tried that?" Toothpick cried wrathfully. "Didn't Jim Stall gather a bunch of his friends, gents who he thought he could trust, an' suggest they start a society of their own an' wipe out the Black Hawks? Didn't every one there swear to hold their tongue, an' didn't they find Jim hangin' to his own front porch the next morning?"

"I savvy. He made a mistake an' took in some friends what was members of the gang."

"Sure, that's the trouble. No one knows who they are. If you start talkin' to some gent private, maybe said gent is one of them buzzards." Toothpick rode on in gloomy silence for a moment. Then he exploded again: "An' old man Hill — You know him; he helped you clean out Stinger an' his gang. He's a tough nut. He tried the same thing, only he didn't have more than six friends at the meeting. They didn't dare tackle the old grizzly in his den, but they sure are raisin' hell with his stock, an' he's lost two of his boys."

Toothpick glanced at Allen, then spat in disgust. He saw that Allen had not even been listening. His nose was twitching, his head cocked to one side like a listening animal, and his strange eyes searched the clump of cotton-woods and red willows ahead.

The trail narrowed as they entered the trees, and Toothpick was forced to drop some distance behind Allen, as the two greys insisted on crowding in directly behind him. They had penetrated the bush but a short distance when Allen suddenly wheeled Princess and swung her into the bushes. As he did so, there came the crack of a heavy rifle, and a bullet whined over their heads.

"Get back!" called Allen.

A volley of shots followed the two as they raced back along the trail. Bullets showered them with leaves. As they left the woods they pulled up.

"Shucks, them gents don't know how to shoot a-tall," grinned Allen. "They couldn't see you, so they must've been after me. Who do you figger they was?"

"Your friends, Kid Moore an' Curly Cole," Toothpick suggested.

"Not any. We been comin' right along, an' there wasn't no dust cloud circlin' us, an' as we left town first, it couldn't have been them." Allen paused and looked quizzically at the lanky puncher. "Guess again."

Toothpick shook his head.

"Reckon some one must have blabbed about me goin' to fetch you."

"Yeah, I reckon they did," Allen said drily.

Toothpick was still puzzling out this remark when he saw Allen's face go white. The little fellow leaped from his saddle and ran to the side of Queen Second, the grey mare with the pack. Her side was covered with blood, her head drooped, and her legs were shaking. Even as he watched, she sank to her knees and rolled over.

"Queenie! Queenie!" Allen's voice grew small and gentle as he spoke to the horse. Then he realized that Queen Second was dead.

"Let's go get the murderin' coyotes!" Toothpick yelled savagely, as he slid from his saddle and yanked his Winchester from its boot.

Allen made no reply, but his face was white and strained. The cords of his neck stood out with the force of the inward struggle. His face was old as he stood there, staring back at the woods. Once he reached out and put his hand on the butt of the Winchester. Toothpick saw the knuckles turn white as the hand clenched it. Then the light went out of Allen's eyes, and his hand fell away.

"Toothpick, I swore I'd never pack a gun again or use a rifle willingly. If they corners me an' I has to fight, then I'll fight. But I ain't cornered, so I reckon we'll circle around to Old Lady Reiker's place." His voice was flat and tired.

Toothpick uttered no word of protest. He knew how Allen loved his horses, and he gathered how terrific had been the struggle to refrain from avenging Queen. He knew, too, the ruthlessness of the Wolf when aroused, and he understood the reason Allen wished to kill that other nature of his.

"Who do you reckon did it?" he asked after they had circled the woods.

"I think I savvy. Maybe I'll tell you in a couple of days. Then you an'" — he hesitated — " that friend of yours, the sheriff, can go gather them in."

CHAPTER
THREE

Old Lady Reiker

It was close to four o'clock when Toothpick Jarrick and Jim-twin Allen topped a rough hogback and looked down at the Double R, Old Lady Reiker's ranch. Everything about it showed the touch of a woman's hand. Neat flower beds brightened the yard; the fences were whitewashed. Curtains fluttered from the upper windows. The place was homelike and inviting, particularly so to men who had ridden many dusty miles under a broiling sun. They put their willing horses into a fast trot down the slope, passed along the lane; and Toothpick pulled up before the house with a flourish.

"Ma Reiker! Ma!" he called. Then he stared at the shuttered windows of the first floor. "What's goin' on here?"

"Sort o' looks as if they was away," said Allen, then he corrected himself: "No, they ain't. They's some one movin' in the house."

Again Toothpick shouted.

This time a curtain jerked in an upper window, a face appeared for a moment, and a woman's voice was heard calling to some one within. Allen slid from his horse and, motioning Toothpick to follow, moved closer to the house so that it would be impossible for any one to fire at them from an upper window.

"Just as well to be on the safe side," he remarked cheerfully.

Toothpick nodded; the two waited close to the door. They heard a scraping noise as of some one moving furniture, then the door was opened a crack.

"That you, Toothpick? Who's that with you? Oh, it's only a boy!" cried a woman's voice, and she threw the door wide open.

A frail little old lady appeared in the opening. Snow-white hair framed her delicate face where finely etched wrinkles added lines of gentle sweetness. She summoned a quavering smile for her visitors, despite the fact that she was obviously tired and worried.

"I was frightened," she explained. "I didn't know it was you."

"This is my friend, Jim Allen." Toothpick waved a hand at "the boy." "Now what does all this mean, Ma?"

"Oh, Toothpick, I'm so glad you came," she sighed. "I'll tell you — But where are my manners? Mr. Allen — mercy, you're not big enough to call mister! Jim, I'm glad to meet you. Now, you two come right in."

"Where are the boys? Where's uncle?" Toothpick stared in amazement at the piles of furniture against the shuttered windows and door. "What's the fuss?"

"The Black Hawks!"

"Them skunks been botherin' you? Why, damn their —"

She interrupted with a smile. "Cussin' won't do any good."

"But what's it all about? Why are you all alone here?"

"The boys got a warning to go, so they went. I don't rightly know what's it about. But the Black Hawks seem to think Bill — that's my brother, Jim Allen — has something they want."

She fluttered over to a desk against one of the windows and took a paper from it which she handed to Toothpick.

"They sent this to Bill."

The puncher read it, then handed it to Allen.

Give it up. Tell us where you hid it, or we will come and make you.

BLACK HAWKS.

"But what is it they want?" asked Toothpick.

Old Lady Reiker hesitated for a moment and glanced doubtfully at Allen. Then she smiled.

"You're Toothpick's friend, and your face is honest," she told him. "I'll talk right ahead. Day before yesterday some one held up the paymaster to the mines and took a lot of money. Bill saw five men standin' around and thinks they were hiding the stolen money. Now they think he went back and got it. Of course, he hasn't got it, so he can't give it up."

Toothpick flashed a glance at Allen, who winked in reply. Both were asking themselves the same question. How did the Black Hawks know they had been spied

26

on by Bill Reiker unless he had returned later and been seen retrieving the money?

"Where's Bill now?" Toothpick asked sharply.

"He went over to ask Mr. Hill if he could stay over there for a while."

"And he left you alone here!" the puncher cried incredulously.

"Oh, no; 'Big Tom' is with me. Anyway, Bill knew they wouldn't hurt me," she cried in warm defence.

"Big Tom!" Toothpick repeated disgustedly. "Who wants Big Tom?"

A huge man, with a bristling walrus moustache, heaved himself through a rear door and glared about. He fairly bristled with weapons. In one hand he held a big Colt and in the other a meat cleaver. Allen winked at Toothpick again. Despite his martial air, Big Tom cast uneasy glances at the door and looked as if he were about to flee for the cellar at any moment.

"Let's put up the hosses; then we can talk things over," Allen suggested.

"Tom, you go help them. You boys must be hungry. There's a fire in the stove, and I'll have supper ready for you by the time you come back." Old Lady Reiker hurried to the kitchen.

"I reckon you know where to find things, Toothpick; there ain't no use my goin' out with you," said Big Tom, with pompous dignity. "You don't have to worry none. Them Black Hawks won't be comin' before night." But they noted that he slammed the front door behind him quickly.

"In all his ton of flesh he ain't got enough nerve to fight one fightin' ant," Toothpick snorted.

"Darn me if Ma Reiker ain't one fine old lady! She's plumb loyal to that brother of hers, an' I'm bettin' he ain't worth a cent," Allen said, as he stripped the saddle from Princess and began to rub her down.

"Not even a plugged cent," agreed Toothpick.

"She makes me feel like blubberin'. Bustlin' around takin' care of folks when she's the most helpless little critter I ever see. An' her alone in that house with the furniture piled against the windows and that big gent hid in the cellar!"

Toothpick grinned to himself as he listened. Allen was unconsciously reverting to type in his sympathy for the weak. When Allen carefully retrieved his rifle from its boot and carried it with him back to the house, the puncher chuckled with delight.

Neither Toothpick nor Allen did much talking during supper. They were too busy eating the many good things set before them.

Big Tom monopolized the conversation with bombastic threats against the Black Hawks.

"I figger they'll think different about attackin' this place when they see a big feller like me protectin' it," he said complacently.

Toothpick gulped a large hunk of corn bread and looked at the Colt and the meat cleaver which Big Tom had placed carefully close beside him on the table.

"I reckon you're faster with the cleaver than they are on the draw," said the tall puncher mildly.

"I reckon I got bigger muscles!" snorted Big Tom.

As though by accident, Toothpick sent a knife clattering to the floor. Instantly Big Tom leaped for the cellar door, betraying an agility remarkable in so huge a mountain of flesh. Jim Allen grinned, but he whispered reprovingly to Toothpick.

"Don't torment him no more. After all, he did stay when the others runned away. And if he's scairt, why it was that much harder for him."

Big Tom returned with an effort to recapture his aplomb.

"Thought I heard somethin' movin' down there," he explained. "Don't you worry none," he patronized Allen. "Even if you are a little feller an' no more nor a boy, Big Tom's here."

Toothpick choked and glanced at Allen, but the small gunman had scarcely heard Big Tom.

"Huh," he said absently.

His eyes, wide and greedy, were fixed on a mammoth pie the old lady had just placed on the table. Her eyes in turn widened as she watched him demolish piece after piece.

"Land's sakes, I'm proud that you like my pie, but I'm scairt you'll bust," she gasped in awe, as he finished his fourth slice.

He flashed her one of his loose, lovable grins. "Missis —"

"My friends call me 'Ma,' " she corrected.

"Ma, I'm admittin' frank that I'm plumb hoggish when I see a pie, an' I sure wish I was bigger so I could hold more," he said regretfully.

Later Toothpick and Allen agreed between themselves that it was impossible for the old lady to remain there that night. The moon would be up about nine, and they decided to take her over to Hill's place. But when they broached the idea to her, she refused positively to go; nor would she give any reason for her refusal. They argued and pleaded in vain. Despite her fragility, she showed a determination that baffled the two men. At last they had to give up.

The best they could do would be to try to defend the house in case the Black Hawks attacked that night. They felt that defence would be hopeless, for the place was too large to be defended successfully by two men against large numbers. Both of them automatically discounted Big Tom being of any aid in the predicament.

"I'll watch outside; you stay here with her," Allen instructed Toothpick. "If I hear anyone comin', I'll give you warning. Two wolf cries, an' you pick her up an' go out the back door. Three cries, an' you go out the front door. Don't mind what she says. If I calls, you pick her up an' start somewhere, 'cause from what I hear of them skunks, they ain't above handlin' her rough if they gets the idea she knows where the money is."

Allen had chosen a time to speak when the old lady was in the kitchen. He grinned cheerfully at her as she returned to the room.

"Don't you worry none," he told her. "Go to bed and sleep easy, 'cause I figger they won't be comin' to-night, an' even if they does, they won't hurt you." He

30

could not resist adding, with a wink at Toothpick: "No, they won't hurt you, but they'll sure skin Big Tom."

The big man glanced about wildly. Old Lady Reiker hastened to his defence, saying: "Jim, you mustn't say such things."

Allen nodded and grinned as he slipped through the door into the night, but when the old lady realized that this boy proposed to remain outside on watch in the darkness, she made a spirited protest.

"I won't think of letting him risk his life. If those wicked men —"

"Don't you worry none about Jim. Him an' them hosses of hisn is worth twenty watchdogs. You trot on to bed," Toothpick urged.

Finally he persuaded her that Jim was in no danger, which, to his own surprise, proved to be true. The night slipped away slowly but uneventfully. The dreaded riders did not come. Much later in the day Allen and Toothpick were to learn the reason; meanwhile they puzzled over it.

"Can't figger out why they let this place alone unless —" Allen paused.

"Unless what, Jim?" asked Toothpick.

"Well, they was aimin' to get Bill Reiker. If they knowed he'd flew this coop —"

Soon after breakfast Allen was saddling his horse to ride over to Hill's ranch and wring the truth from Bill Reiker, when seven horsemen turned into the gate and started toward the house. Allen flung up his rifle intending to drop a shot before them as a warning to halt. Then he recognized the man at their head. With a whoop of joy he started forward to meet them. The leader in turn saw him and spurred forward, pulled up beside him and leaned down to wring his hand.

"Gee, I'm glad to see you, Mr. Hill!" Allen cried.

"Kid, you're sure a pleasant sight yourself!"

Allen knew several of Hill's riders, and they crowded about him. Then Hill and Allen walked to the house, and the punchers followed.

"How come you rode over here, Mr. Hill?" Allen asked.

"Come to get Mrs. Reiker — she can't stay alone here," explained Hill. "I was to town last night, an' when I get back this mornin' I find that sneakin' brother of hers hidin' over to my place. When I hears what he has to say, I comes a-running over here."

"Well, it was peaceful enough here last night," said Allen. "Wonder if the Black Hawks knows he's over to your ranch."

Hill could not enlighten him on that.

"We tried to get Mrs. Reiker to go over to your place last night when we was expectin' trouble, but a mule ain't nothing to that woman when she gets set," Allen went on. "She refused to go flat. You'd think you was aimin' to poison her."

Hill chuckled and said sheepishly: "It's this way, Jim. Now don't you bust out laughin', or I'll take you apart to see what makes you go. I'm courtin' Martha Reiker, an' I reckon she wouldn't come 'cause she figgered it warn't proper without a chaperon."

"I ain't never seed two folks that would make a better pair than you two," said Allen sincerely.

32

He smiled as he noted how the old lady blushed as shyly as a girl when she saw Hill. She still protested against leaving her own home, but when Hill told her that his housekeeper was expecting her, she consented to go. Her especial treasures and herself were packed into a wagon, driven by Big Tom; and, escorted by Hill and his riders, the procession set out for Hill's ranch.

Old Lady Reiker cast a look back at her homey, pleasant ranch house.

"You don't reckon them Black Hawks'll take their spite out on the buildings, do you?" she asked tremulously.

"We got to risk it," said Hill. "We can't spare enough men to watch it. Anyways, I figger they're after what they think Bill's got, not the house itself. Moreover," he added, giving her a sly glance, "maybe you'll be takin' a new home afore long."

Old Lady Reiker blushed and looked down at her little hands, primly folded in their black-lace mitts.

CHAPTER
FOUR

Allen Follows Trail

When they reached the main road and headed toward Hill's ranch, the old man disposed of his forces much as he would have done in Indian times. He sent two men to ride far ahead of the main body and act against a possible surprise. It was well on the cards that the Black Hawks might attempt an attack. Both Hill and the Reikers were under their ban.

Allen and Toothpick exchanged sly grins as they watched the old warrior play the Lothario. He rode beside the wagon and talked to the old lady. Several times Hill caught their grins, and his desperate efforts to ignore them only added to their amusement. At last he could endure it no longer; he reined in his horse until the two caught up with him.

"Wipe them grins out, you two apes, or I'm goin' on the warpath pronto," he threatened.

Allen continued to grin impudently and hummed softly: "I'm goin' to be married in June."

Hill snorted and made a reach for Allen, but the moment his arm started, Allen ducked, kneed his grey and was a yard out of reach before Hill's hand arrived at the place he had been. Toothpick chuckled; instantly the old man's left hand shot out, caught the lanky puncher by the arm, and nearly yanked him from the saddle.

"Just 'cause Jim here is quick like a cat and makes me look like a bogged buffalo ain't no sign the old man has slowed up complete, you long-legged, red-headed galoot!"

Hill, having demonstrated that, even if he was slow as compared to Allen, he was still not altogether on the shelf, was restored to good humour. He grew thoughtful and gazed at Allen speculatively.

"Jim, when you move quick like that, it shows me why you was so damned sure with them guns of yours."

The three rode on in silence for a moment; then Hill turned to Toothpick and said: "You go tell them fellows what is ridin' ahead to watch careful at them trees by the fork."

Toothpick knew that this was but an excuse to get rid of him; he spurred forward without argument and joined the advance guard.

"A hell of a long time ago I laid aside my guns like you've done, Jim," said the old man. "I got so good that I found myself goin' huntin' for gunmen to test my skill against. I talked to myself plain 'cause I seen I was gettin' the urge to kill. I figgered I could keep on and become a real killer or put away my guns. Is that why you laid aside yours?"

"No, it warn't that," Allen replied. "I got plumb tired havin' folks figure I was no good except to down some gent. Some one gets in trouble an' he sends for the Wolf to help him an' gun a couple of gents. I gets plumb tired of playin' wolf, so I quits." Allen was thoughtful for a moment. "An' I was gettin' more like a real wolf each time I done it, an' then there was another reason, too."

"Son, I knows how you feel, but you never drew steel except to help some lunatic what was gettin' set upon, an' you never downed no gent what didn't need killin' bad."

"Yeah, but just the same, I'm through."

"An' that other reason — was Snippets MacPherson?"

"Yeah. I knows she's as far away as the moon, but just the same I ain't aimin' to have her think of me like a gent does a hangman," Allen said flatly.

Hill glanced at Allen's face; it was as old and tired as his own. One man was sixty, the other not yet thirty; but the younger man had lived through so much that his spirit was far the older, and his face in repose showed that.

They passed through a bunch of aspens and in and out of a crisscross of dry gulches. Then Allen pointed first straight ahead of them, then to the right and the left.

"What you make of them dust clouds?" he asked Hill. "Sort o' looks as if the ones on the sides is cuttin' in on the centre one, an' all three is hurryin' some."

Hill squinted until he caught the faint white haze of dust clouds against the blue sky.

" 'Tain't my boys," he muttered. "I tol' three of 'em to circle in the Whisperin' Hills an' the rest to stay put at the ranch. Sort o' looks, whoever them gents are, as

36

if they don't belong on my range. They're about five miles away. Must be close to Bear Bluff."

The two watched the dust clouds race toward each other and finally merge into one. The single cloud stood still for about five minutes, then moved more slowly toward the northwest.

"What you make of it?" asked the old man.

"Dunno. It's sort o' queer. They was all hittin' the high spots until they comes together, then they moves slow. Didn't hear no shots, so I can't figure them gents what was cuttin' in on t'others was hostile, or there would sure have been a little shootin'. No gent is givin' up in this valley without makin' a little play."

Hill frowned. He knew one man cowardly enough to give in to one man, much less four or five, without daring to make a play.

"Jim, I got an idea. There's reasons I don't want to spill it yet, but I'm worried. I'm goin' to tell Big Tom to hustle that wagon along. Leave four men with it, an' you an' me an' the rest will sort o' hustle an' investigate."

He cast an anxious glance at the old lady. Allen divined what was troubling him. From what he had heard of Bill Reiker, Allen understood that he was a miserable specimen; he was the one man in the valley who would surrender without an attempt to fight. He realized that it was possible the Black Hawks had captured their man and were carrying him away to extract information from him.

37

The trail from their present position to Bear Bluff ran across a flat table-land which offered no concealment for a possible enemy. There was no chance of an attack on the wagon. Hill reassured Old Lady Reiker and ordered four men to remain with her. Then he and the rest of the riders with Allen spurred straight toward Bear Bluff. They raced to within a thousand yards of it, then halted while Allen slipped on ahead to scout the intervening rough country.

Half an hour passed, then a wolf howl rang out, and they galloped on again. They found Allen standing beside the trail. He motioned the punchers to stay back while Hill and Toothpick joined him alone on foot. To them he pointed out various signs on the road and along the sides. Much of what he pointed out was invisible to their eyes. It had not rained for several weeks, and the ground was hard and dry, but they realized that Allen knew whereof he spoke.

"Three gents comes from the east and two from the west, and one comes from your ranch. One of the five gets here ahead of the others, an' I figger he ropes the gent what was comin' from your ranch. You can see where a gent made a dent in the ground. But he warn't hurt much, 'cause he got up on his feet later. I figger them five gents catched this one comin' from your ranch, an' I reckon we knows who he was."

"Why didn't they gun the coyote instead of ropin' him?" growled Hill.

"This sure explains why they didn't raid the ranch last night," said Allen. "They must have knowed they'd get him here. Now what you aimin' to do?"

38

"He's got that stolen loot. Let 'em make him tell where it is."

"But suppose he don't know where it is, after all. The way I figger it, them gents, if he don't know — Well, that future brother-in-law of yours won't be lookin' human when they finish with him."

"Hell, there ain't nothin' to do but go an' get him back!" Toothpick cried in disgust.

"We got to do it for the old lady," Allen said quickly. "It would bust her heart if she ever seed her brother after them animals works on him."

"All right, stop jawin' an' let's get started," groaned Toothpick.

Allen grinned and shook his head.

"You got to remember them gents ain't babies. They sure see our dust cloud an' they figger maybe we'll come tearin' along after them. They'll leave a trail plain for a kid to read. Then when you start readin' it, they'll wait in a handy place an' shoot hell out of you."

"What's to be done, then?" asked Hill.

But Toothpick sensed Allen's plan before he answered and objected promptly.

"Not on your life, Jim. You ain't trailin' them by your lonesome."

Allen ignored him and addressed Hill.

"Reckon me an' Princess can follow 'em without raisin' dust. I figger they'll leave a plain trail for maybe ten miles, an' then start to muss it up. I follow an' when I toll 'em, I'll give you a signal an' you boys come a-whoopin'. You savvy Indian talk, Mr. Hill?"

"Yep."

"Then you keep watch over to the northwest, an' I'll give you Indian talk with a mirror which way they went."

Allen fashioned a hackamore with his rope for the head of the grey colt; then he handed the end to Toothpick.

"She's plumb young an' shuffles her feet," he explained. "You hand her to Snippets to-morrow."

Toothpick cursed as he took the rope. He knew that Allen thought there was a chance he would not return to present the mare himself. Quickly he unbuckled his belt and holster and offered it to Allen.

"If you're set on makin' a damn fool of yourself, take this with you."

"Nope. I ain't wearin' guns," Allen said cheerfully.

Princess trotted away along the trail left by the captors of Bill Reiker. All watched the little gunman until he vanished down the draw; then they rode back to Old Lady Reiker and resumed the march to the ranch.

CHAPTER
FIVE

The Rescue

Hill's ranch house was an unattractive place. It had been erected with an eye for defence rather than beauty in the days when Indians menaced the valley. Its house, barns, and bunk houses formed a hollow square with a small court on the inside. It was a squat, thick-walled affair and stood in the centre of a large clearing, barren of bushes and trees. There was not a spot about it which could be used as cover by an enemy.

When Hill led Mrs. Reiker into the house, the old lady looked about her and sniffed with a tidy woman's disapproval of man's disorder. The Irish woman whom Hill had hired to remain at the ranch and clean it before the old lady's arrival had started her cleaning operations, unfortunately, in the rear, so Mrs. Reiker beheld the living room in its native state of chaotic disorder.

"Land's sakes!" The old lady threw up her hands in horror. "I'm going to start straightening up this room right this moment."

Hill gave his assent to her cleaning operations without a protest, and in so doing he also bade farewell to his happy-go-lucky bachelor days, though he did not realize it. That room had decided the old lady; Hill needed taking care of.

Toothpick was in a fever of impatience. The moment Hill fled the dust of Mrs. Reiker's efficient broom and appeared in the open, the puncher rushed up to him and pleaded:

"Look-a-here, Mr. Hill, let's plant a man on top of Bear Bluff what savvies Indian talk an' you and me follow that trail as long as it's plain. We keeps in sight of that bluff at the same time. Then when the gent there gets Allen's talk, he flashes it to us an' we is that much nearer."

After a moment's thought Hill agreed to the plan. He with Toothpick and six heavily armed riders and two lookouts rode to the foot of the bluff. When the two lookouts had climbed to the crest of the bluff, the rest started to follow the trail of the five kidnappers. As Allen had said, the trail was easily followed; twice it led through narrow gaps in the hills. In each instance they saw signs that the kidnappers had prepared traps. They had galloped through the gaps at high speed, then doubled back on foot. The marks proved they had remained in hiding there for some time.

The trail was clear as far as Muddy Creek; there it was obvious the men had entered the water. But try as they could, none of the pursuers could pick up the trail again after that. About a hundred yards up the creek, the banks were hardpan, and it was probable that the quarry had left the creek there, but none could determine whether they had headed north or south. At last, one of the riders found a long mark scratched in the hardpan. It was an arrow, pointing almost due south. Beneath, they deciphered the words:

Split in twos. Watch Lookout Rock.

"If I didn't know the darn little runt I'd say he was guessin', but if he says they split in twos I reckon they did," said Hill.

One of the riders crawled back and forth across the hardpan striving to find the trail; at last he arose to his feet and spat in disgust.

"If he saw signs hereabout, his eyes ain't human."

"They ain't," said Toothpick shortly.

They laid a rough course toward Lookout Rock which would allow them to watch Bear Bluff at the same time. But they were forced to halt at last because they were going it blind, and it was possible they were headed in the wrong direction. The sun was low in the sky before they received the impatiently waited signal. It flashed first from the peak of Lookout Rock, then from Bear Bluff. Hill and two old-timers among the riders had no difficulty in reading the message, but to Toothpick and the others it was so much gibberish.

"Reckon he must mean Stinger Moore's place," Hill said.

"An' we ain't to come close till dark," an old-timer added. "That there last long sweep was the sun."

"Didn't get that, but I reckon you're right," Hill assented.

The crescent moon's pale light did little to relieve the darkness when they moved forward. Toothpick felt the pulse beat in his throat as they went on in single file. The men they were to attack were hard fighters and desperate. Even Hill found his heart beating a little faster; he sighed with content as the spirit of adventure again coursed through his aged body.

Suddenly they heard a wolf call almost directly before them; pressing forward, they found Allen awaiting them at the entrance through a thick mass of mesquite brush which surrounded Stinger Moore's place.

"You come up quick," Allen greeted.

"We didn't wait for your signal. We started trailin' you pronto," Hill explained.

"Reckoned you would."

"Where are they?"

"Up in Stinger's old house. Better leave a couple of men here with the hosses to act as guards. The rest come along careful," Allen directed.

Cautiously the men made their way down the lane on foot and crept toward the light that marked the house. They separated, and two men went to each window while the rest moved toward the door. Toothpick peered through a window and saw Bill Reiker bound to a chair. His face was ghastly white, and his eyes stared in horror at a man who was heating a poker in the stove. Toothpick started when the man with the poker raised his head. It was Curly Cole. Four other men sprawled in chairs, laughing, talking and smoking. Obviously they were jeering and taunting the terror-stricken prisoner.

"You tellin' or you goin' to make me work over you with this?"

Curly Cole held up the red-hot poker.

"No, no. I tol' you the truth. I saw five men hide something over in Coffin Gulch, an' I went back later to see what it was an' it was gone," Bill Reiker wailed.

"Why did you run when you see me?"

" 'Cause I thought you was the man what had dug up the money and I was scared," moaned the prisoner.

"You thought Curly dug it up?" interrupted one of the men.

All four cast suspicious glances at Curly. All knew that they themselves would have double-crossed him if given the chance; therefore they believed instinctively that he might have tricked them. Curly sprang toward Reiker with an oath; the captive squirmed in his bonds and screamed in a paroxysm of terror. Then came a loud knock on the door, and a voice shouted:

"Hands up, you fellows in there!"

At the same moment the glass in both windows splintered; guns and men's faces filled the openings. For a split second the men in the room remained like statues; then Curly, with a swift movement, sent his poker crashing against the lamp. A flare of red flame, and the room was in darkness. Instantly the men outside dropped below the sills.

"Curly Cole!" called Allen.

"That you, Jim Allen?" Curly's voice was plainly astonished.

"Yep."

"Where did you come from?"

"Been sittin' on your tails all day. And you gents think you are trackers!" Allen taunted.

"You try to come in here an' the first man I drop will be Bill Reiker," Curly threatened.

"That ain't no skin off o' my foot, but I'm tellin' you plain if you does you'll hang sure. I'm givin' you a minute to come out, an' if you don't I'll fire the house."

"If you does, Bill Reiker will frizzle alive!" Curly added a curse while he racked his brain desperately for a chance to escape.

"You ain't got much time left," Allen called.

Bill Reiker began to scream hysterical curses at both the rescue party and Curly; then he begged first one, then the other, to save him.

"They got us sure. That damn Wolf won't let us off to save a dozen cowardly curs like that skunk in the chair," Curly whispered to his friends.

"Yeah, I knows him. He'd burn the lot of us alive an' laugh when we start fryin'. Damn him!" one of the men whispered back.

"What happens if we give up?" Curly demanded aloud.

"We take you to Beaverville an' turn you over to the sheriff."

Curly hesitated; for a moment he doubted that he had heard a right.

"You promise that?"

"Yep!"

"Then I'm comin' out. You're the Wolf, but you're fool enough to keep your promise!"

A light flared up in the hall; one by one the five marched out with their hands up and were disarmed and bound. Allen whispered to Hill to mark the guns. As Allen was tying one of the men's hands his vest fell open and Curly saw that there was no concealed weapon beneath it.

"You warn't armed yesterday?" he asked.

Allen grinned and shook his head.

"Hell, an' I didn't blow you apart!" Curly regretted. After that he lapsed into a brooding silence.

The instant Bill Reiker was freed from his bonds, he rushed at Allen and shook his fist in his face.

"You — you would have let me burn!" he shouted.

"I sure would if you hadn't been your sister's brother," Allen said coolly.

Toothpick pushed the half-crazed man away and thrust him out the front door.

"Get outside and be yourself. If it hadn't been for him, you'd look like a zebra now."

It was close to three o'clock when they returned to Hill's ranch with their prisoners. Despite the late hour, they found Old Lady Reiker dozing in a chair awaiting them. The instant she saw Bill, she ran to him and cried out her relief.

"Bill, are you all right? I couldn't figger why the men all rid away an' you wasn't here to the ranch house. Was you in danger?"

"Yeah, an' small thanks to them I got out of it," growled Bill ungraciously, with a venomous glance at Allen.

Hill told the old lady in a few words the story of Bill's capture, leaving out the part about the hot poker, which would have upset her too much.

"That's the way you makes it out," grumbled Reiker. "Makes yourself out all heroes, in especial him." He indicated Allen contemptuously.

Old Lady Reiker flushed uneasily at her brother's words. At her first opportunity she called Allen aside.

"You mustn't mind him, Jim," she said anxiously. "He had a hard time and isn't himself. To-morrow he'll be sorry. I'm awful grateful to you for what you done."

"Shucks, ma'am, 'tain't nothin' a-tall. I don't know what you is spoutin' about," Allen laughed.

The following morning at dawn, Allen and Toothpick started for Beaverville with the prisoners. The latter were unbound, but each was fastened to the other by a rope about the neck.

"I'm sort o' hopin' one of you coyotes will make a break," Toothpick told them grimly.

"Hell, you ain't got nothin' agin' us," laughed one.

"Jim, them coyotes is plumb lucky. Why in hell didn't they give us a chance to shoot them up?" Toothpick grumbled. "Their trial will be a stacked deck, an' they'll be out in a month, 'cause them Black Hawks will get on the jury an' turn them loose. We won't have gained nothin'."

"You're wrong, kid. We'll have gained a lot."

"How come?"

"To-morrow or next day, you just add two and two and see if they don't make four." Allen laughed aloud at Toothpick's perplexed face.

When they reached the town, a crowd swarmed after them; as they made their way to the jail, a few jeered at the prisoners. They marched the five into the sheriff's office, where they found him and one of his deputies.

"Hullo, Curly! What you been up to?" asked Duff Dorwin. Then, without waiting for an answer, he turned to Allen. "'Lo, Jim! You did show up after all. You owe me a drink."

"Sure, I'll pay it just as soon as I get loose from these coyotes." Allen's nonchalance matched the sheriff's.

"We ain't done nothin', Duff," one of the men growled.

"Nope, not a thing except kidnappin'," said Allen. "Also attempted torture, suspicion of bein' mixed up in the last pay-roll robbery, an' —"

"What's that?" The sheriff leaped to his feet.

A crowd of curious men clustered in the doorway and he strode forward to slam the door in their faces, but Allen put out a hand and stopped him.

"Shucks, let 'em hear about it. I ain't scared to back up my talk afore the whole town," he said easily.

For a moment the little gunman's eyes clashed with those of the sheriff; then Dorwin turned and sat down again.

"Why for do you figure they was mixed up in the pay-roll robbery?" he asked.

"Bill Reiker seed 'em buryin' the loot. He went back to try an' get it, an' Curly spotted him. When Curly looked for the stuff, it was gone. Of course, I don't know what Curly was doin' back there alone."

A rumbling growl rose from the prisoners as they glared at Curly. Curly's eyes were those of a mad animal as he faced Allen.

"I'll kill you for that," he snarled.

Allen ignored him.

"Course I don't know if Curly intended to double-cross his pals, but anyway, when he looked for the stuff it was gone an' he thinks Bill Reiker took it. But he's plumb mistook, 'cause it was gone when Reiker got there. Reckon another member of the gang played the double-cross afore Curly got there."

Again Curly mouthed threats against Allen, and again the others grumbled curses. But Allen was watching the sheriff; Dorwin's face was a cold, hard mask.

"So I'm accusin' these gents of the pay-roll robbery, of kidnappin' Bill Reiker," Allen went on, "attempted murder an' torture an' a whole lot more. I heard 'em talkin' about it. So did Reiker. I figger we got enough to lock 'em up for." He turned to Toothpick. "Go get their guns."

The sheriff and his deputy hustled the prisoners through a back door into the cell block. When Duff Dorwin returned, Allen pointed to the sack of rifles and Colts which Toothpick had placed on a desk.

"There are their weapons." He moved toward the door, then swung about and added genially: "I 'most forgot. I finds Black Hawk dresses an' hoods in the room with them. I reckon if they ain't Black Hawks, they was pretendin' to be. Come on, I'll buy you that drink now."

"Another time," the sheriff said throatily.

He sat sunk in the chair for five minutes after Allen left; then he leaped to his feet and went to Curly Cole's cell.

"Damn you, you made a hell of a mess of things!" The genial, suave sheriff was gone; Duff Dorwin's heavy face was livid with rage.

"You wouldn't talk that way if I had a gun," Curly told him coldly.

"You fool, you think I'm scared of you and your gun. You're good until you're up against a man with nerve. Damn you, what a mess you've made!"

"Me! And who thought it would be smart to ask Allen to come here, I'd like to know?" Curly retorted furiously.

"Shut up! You know damn well Toothpick was goin' to get him anyway. When I couldn't stop Toothpick seein' him, I had to pretend to want him to come. Damn that long-legged galoot. I'd like to know how he got through that pass without my seein' him!"

"I suppose that was my fault, too," sneered Curly. Then he added suspiciously: "You know who lifted that loot?"

"Ain't you got any brains a-tall? How could I know. Wasn't I on my way back from seein' that cussed Wolf when the stuff was dug up?"

"Then it was Kid Moore or Sam Speil!" Curly cried.

"That ain't the important thing now. We got to get rid of that Wolf pronto, 'cause I know he's on to me. Damn him, he looks at you an' reads what's inside your head. Now we got to call a meeting an' have him condemned. After that — Now, you listen." Dorwin lowered his voice and whispered earnestly to Curly for several minutes.

When he finished, Curly grinned and agreed. "That ought to do it."

"He won't do it for me, 'cause he sure knows where I stand, but if I has several old-timers who he knows along with me, I reckon he'll either come with us or follow us, an', to get to Land's End, he's got to take the trail through Dry Wash. That's where you come in. And don't mess things up again," the sheriff ended earnestly.

Curly's reply was positive.

"Just let me catch him on my sights, an' there won't be no Wolf!"

CHAPTER
SIX

The Posse

The following day Hill, Toothpick, and Allen were stretched luxuriously in the shade of the ranch-house porch. They were full to repletion with Old Lady Reiker's unexcelled food. Cigarettes dangled from their lips; they were content.

"You ain't really goin', Jim?" Hill asked.

"Yeah, I reckon I'll slide out to-night."

"Well, afore you go, suppose you tell what Mike the bartender tol' you yesterday," urged Toothpick.

"You ever asked Mike to spill anythin' to you?" asked Allen.

"Yeah, lots of times. He wouldn't say nothin' a-tall."

"Why wouldn't he tell you?"

"The darned fool said I talked too much, that I couldn't keep nothin' to myself," said the lanky puncher aggrievedly.

"He was right, wasn't he?"

Toothpick gasped. "What do you mean?"

"Didn't you promise to say nothin' to nobody about my even talkin' to Mike?"

"Sure I did, but Mr. Hill here —"

Allen interrupted: "Is Mr. Hill nobody? Sure, I know he's square an' my friend, but when I say nobody, I mean nobody."

Toothpick pondered on this for a moment and scratched his head.

"Reckon you're right," he admitted gloomily.

"Don't be forgettin'. Nobody means nobody, an' if Mike gets gunned or strung up, it'll be up to you to pay for the funeral, 'cause you'll have caused it."

Toothpick reddened and was silent. He felt crestfallen and hurt. Allen's rebuke was justified but he felt he had been too severe.

"Ain't there nothin' you can tell without breakin' your word nor causin' trouble, Jim?" asked Hill.

"Mr. Hill, I didn't learn nothin' yesterday I didn't know," Allen said frankly. "The thing is plumb simple. It's darned funny, but if you give some folks a ribbon or a feather to stick in their hats or dress 'em up different than other folks, they plumb lose what little brains they got an' believe things an' do things they never would think of otherwise. There has been other societies like these here Black Hawks. Some of them done good an' some done bad. Sort o' depended on who the leaders was. Now these Black Hawks is bein' used. A gang of bad ones squirmed their way to the top.

"They rob trains and pay rolls, rustle cattle, then lay the blame on some rival gang of outlaws — an' the Black Hawks go out an' virtuously hang 'em or drive 'em out of the country. Then the Black Hawks go home feelin' they done right by their civic duty. They ain't bad, they're just dumb. If a gent gets suspicious or

54

maybe spots one of them rustlin' cows, the gang what is runnin' the show calls a meetin', and the virtuous Black Hawks go out an' tar an' feather him."

"Sure, all that's plain as the nose on your face," Hill assented.

"What I'm gettin' at is this — the Black Hawks couldn't do what they does unless they had a couple of gents minglin' with the decent folks an' shoutin': 'Down with the Black Hawks!' Jim Stall gets ten of his friends together to start cleanin' out the Black Hawks. They all swears to keep dumb, but he gets hung the next day. Mr. Hill, you asked six of your friends to talk about the same thing. The day after, the Black Hawks declare war on you. Some one who was a secret Black Hawk betrayed both you an' Stall. Remember the names of the ten he had, 'cause you was there? And the six you had? Well, I'd be darned suspicious of any gent what was at both meetings."

Hill's brow puckered as he went over the two lists of names. Then he started and swore to himself.

"I've been a damn fathead!" he cried.

"Shucks, it ain't fat," Allen grinned. "It's your fool idea that every man is honest until proved otherwise. If a gent appears open and frank, you accept him as that. Now, me, I don't believe no one even when they prove they're honest. You take this gent we're both thinkin' of; he comes here and talks frank and open. He helps you clean out a bunch of two-by-four rustlers and tinhorn gamblers, an' you all fall for him like hot cakes.

"He wears his gun on the right side an' he ain't fast on the draw, so you figures he ain't no gunman what is in hidin'. Now, you let me tell you somethin'. I'll bet you Princess agin' a doughnut that the reason that there gent ain't fast with his right hand is because he's left-handed. An' I'll bet he packs another gun in a shoulder holster to use if he has to be fast. From the way he coils his rope and cinches his hoss, I'll bet he comes from Wyoming way, an' my brother Jack would sure know him pronto. If you don't believe me, you wire Jack an' ask him."

"I'll do that," Hill snapped. "I want to be sure."

"Someone's comin', an' you'll have to stop your jawin'," Toothpick announced.

"Yeah, I've been watchin' that cloud for half an hour. Must be seven or eight gents, an' they're comin' fast," Allen said indifferently.

Ten minutes later seven men streaked out of the wash and headed across the opening for the ranch house. Their horses were blown and sweat covered, telling of a hard ride. At their head rode Duff Dorwin, the sheriff.

"Shucks, they come to tell us their prisoners have escaped," laughed Allen.

The men pulled up their sweating horses close to the house and dismounted in a cloud of dust. The sheriff advanced toward the porch, beating the dust from his hat and shoulders as he came.

"Howdy, Mr. Hill. 'Lo, you two. Ain't seen five gents what was in a pesky hurry, have you?"

"Who's they?" asked Toothpick innocently.

"Curly Cole an' that bunch of his. They filed away the bars an' made a clean get-away." The sheriff addressed Hill, but watched Allen from the corner of his eyes.

The members of the posse crowded up to the porch; Hill greeted most of them as friends. Three of the older men stared at Allen; then they advanced, wrung his hands, and showered him with questions. All were obviously delighted to see him again.

"Hello, Jim, I'm plumb tickled to see you. Heard tell you was somewhere in the valley. You goin' to help clean —" The speaker glanced about hastily and fell silent. It was poor policy to talk about the Black Hawks even in the midst of supposed friends.

"Nope, I ain't helpin' clean nothin'," Allen answered the unspoken question. "I'm pullin' out this evenin'."

The sheriff glanced at him sharply. Was this the truth? He decided that Allen was lying for purposes of his own; thus he made his second mistake in his estimate of the little gunman.

"We figure someone outside must have slipped them files in," one of the posse explained. "When Hogan, the jailer, came with their breakfast this mornin', the bars were cut and they was clean away."

"We tracked 'em to the White Sands and then we lost them complete," said another. "But there ain't no doubt they're headin' for Land's End, 'cause they could get supplies from their friends there an' there's a hell of a lot of rough country t'other side of them hills."

"I don't figure they're headin' for Land's End. I think they aim to switch toward the Bad Lands," the sheriff cut in impatiently. "If they once get in there, it would take a million men to get them out. Let's cut the talk. I'm the sheriff an' in charge," he added firmly.

"Nobody's sayin' you're not, but we all knows this country better than you," one of the posse persisted stubbornly.

The sheriff shrugged and turned to Hill.

"We want fresh hosses an' some grub. Then we'll be on our way."

Hill shouted for his foreman, who promptly rounded up fresh horses and changed the saddles while the men gulped down their food in the bunk house. As they ate, they continued their argument.

"Why for don't you circle through Dry Wash an' if you don't hit nothin' keep goin' over to Stinger Moore's old place an' then on to the Bad Lands?" Allen suggested mildly.

"That's the ticket. What say, sheriff?"

"Waste too much time. I tell you I'm positive they've gone over to the Bad Lands. They can't get supplies at Stinger's old place," snapped the sheriff.

"By gum, sheriff, I got an idea!" cried one of the old-timers enthusiastically. "Jim Allen here is better than a bloodhound when it comes to trackin'. Why not ask him to come along?"

The sheriff grew sullen. "Reckon I can track them coyotes."

"Sure, you're good, but you ain't like Allen," the other persisted.

"The posse is big enough as it is," Dorwin replied, with a well-simulated frown.

As the men drifted outside, the argument grew more heated. The older members were incensed at what they considered the sheriff's obstinacy; they thought he was allowing his pride to interfere with his duty by not deputizing Allen instantly and insisting that he help track the fugitives. At last the sheriff flung up his hands in a helpless gesture and jumped on his horse.

"All right. Johnson, you take Dick Williams an' Pete Simpson an' circle through Dry Wash like Allen says, an' see what you find. If you strike anything, shoot off your guns an' we'll come a-runnin'. We'll leave word which way we've gone."

He galloped across the clearing and vanished down the draw, followed by the other three members. The remaining three climbed to their horses soberly. They did not like the idea of attempting to pick up the fugitives by themselves. It would mean five against three. The five were desperate men, and the three were old and weakened by soft living.

They pleaded and urged Allen to go with them, but he refused resolutely. He insisted that he had nothing against Curly and the others; he would not help in tracking them down. He advised them to follow the sheriff and not attempt to find the fugitives by themselves.

At last they decided to take his advice and they spurred their horses to follow Dorwin.

Hill bit off a big piece of chewing tobacco and said admiringly: "Jim, you sure hit the nail on the head that time."

"You get what your friend was after?" Allen asked, with a broad grin. "He had me guessin' for a time, but I figger I got his number now."

Hill frowned. "I don't get you."

"You talkin' more riddles?" jeered Toothpick.

"How many trails through Dry Wash?" Allen asked.

"One."

"And she sure turns and twists, don't she?"

"She sure does."

"An' is chock-full of boulders and nice places for a dry gulcher," Hill cut in. A glimmering of the truth was coming to him.

"An' our friend sure made it plain he wanted to go toward the Bad Lands," Allen continued.

"Which if you was on to him, would sort o' make you believe he was leadin' the pursuit away on a false trail on purpose," Hill rejoined quickly.

"An' in consequence, if I thought he was lyin' I might lead them there through Dry Wash."

"Yeah, and if you did, there'd be five waitin' for you there. He was sure actin' an' tryin' to make you run your neck into a noose," Hill agreed.

"Shucks, what the hell is you gents talkin' about? If Jim thinks them gents is headed toward Land's End, why in hell not go get them?" Toothpick complained.

Allen grinned sarcastically.

"Ain't you never growed up? Can't you add two and two?"

"Damn you for a little piebald runt. You said the same thing yesterday," Toothpick snorted.

"Shucks, lets me an' you go play Indians with them gents in Dry Wash," Allen suggested. "We'll work around 'em an' scare 'em a bit."

"Sort o' dangerous fun!" Hill warned.

"Yeah, that's why it's fun," said Allen.

He started with Toothpick for the corral and bunk houses where the punchers were preparing for the beef round-up. But in the short walk Allen reconsidered. The sheriff had thrown down a challenge, and he hated to let it go. In the old days he would have gone hunting the men who were waiting to ambush him. Now it was different. If he went, it would be simply to prove that he could not be trapped. That seemed foolish.

"Reckon I'm too tired for that trip after all," he said.

"Shucks, you ain't even good for funnin' no more," snorted the irate Toothpick.

CHAPTER
SEVEN

Snippets

An hour later, Toothpick and Allen wandered back to the porch. Old Lady Reiker came bustling out to meet them. Her cheeks were flushed, and she wore the mysterious air of the bearer of important news. She smiled knowingly at Allen.

"I have a caller. Guess who it is!" she whispered.

Allen shook his head; then he caught sight of two saddled horses before the ranch house. He stared at their brands, then flushed and looked about quickly. The horses were both from the Bar II Bar. Allen looked back to the old lady, an eager question in his eyes. She laughed and pointed into the house.

A girl's clear voice came from the living room. Then Snippets MacPherson appeared in the doorway. She was as slender as a boy, and her simple grey blouse and corduroy skirt added to the resemblance; but the gay kerchief at her throat and her soft, oval face, with its becoming touch of tan, were distinctly and attractively feminine. Her brown eyes widened and then faltered as she saw Allen. For a long moment the two stared at each other, wordless.

Then she smiled and held out her hand; Allen took it.

"Gosh, it's Snippets," he mumbled, with a poor attempt at appearing casual.

"'Lo Jim." She, too, tried to be casual.

Old Lady Reiker beckoned to Toothpick, and the two went into the house quietly; though as Toothpick observed: "We might shoot off guns, an' even Jim wouldn't hear us now."

Snippets MacPherson had once saved Jim-twin Allen from capture while he lay helpless from wounds. Later, Allen had been of great service to both Snippets and her father.

"I heard you were in the valley," the girl said softly. "I came over to see you as soon as I heard."

"That's fine." Allen shuffled his feet and looked at the floor. "I was comin' over to see you, too. I got a present for you."

"You have!"

"Yeah, I hears you was gettin' hitched, so —"

"Jim, that's not true," she interrupted earnestly. "I told him a week ago I — I wouldn't marry him. I sent him away."

Her brown eyes were fixed on Allen; in them lay a straight-forward question. Snippets was a frank and forthright young person; the White Wolf had changed for her from a romantic hero to a lovable man who meant more to her than any of the suitors who came wooing her, and she wanted him to know it.

Allen realized her meaning. For an instant, his face lighted up and he took a step toward her. Then he stopped short; the light left his face, and it was suddenly old. He had fought out this battle before. A gulf wide as the space between worlds lay between them. He was an outlaw with a price on his head. He could not ask Snippets to share the long trail with him; no, not though she would do it gladly. He strove for a grin and managed to produce a poor imitation of his usual loose smile.

"You forgot how to whistle for the greys?" he asked her abruptly.

Snippets bit her lip. She knew how Allen felt, knew from the firm look in his eyes that there was no arguing with him. She could only accept his verdict.

She tried to smile back at him. Then she placed her hands over her mouth and gave two long, shrill whistles. There came the pounding of hoofs, and Princess, followed by the grey colt, flashed around the corner of the house. They slid to a stop, pricked up their ears, and looked at Allen. Then both wrinkled back their lips and snapped.

"Still the same old greedy Princess," laughed Snippets. "Oh, that colt! What a beauty!"

"That's your present!" said Allen.

Snippets ran to the colt. At first it backed away, but at a word from Allen, it stood rigid. Snippets caressed the soft nose.

"That colt's smart. She'll do everything that Princess will do an' more, too," Allen said proudly.

Snippets saddled the colt and tried out its paces. The more she rode, the greater grew her delight. A tall

64

puncher shambled around the corner of the ranch house and stood watching her.

"That's a right fine hoss, Snippets," he observed nasally. "Reckon we better be gettin' started home."

Toothpick and the old lady came out on the porch. Snippets dismounted and said her good-byes, with a kiss for the old lady. At the last she turned to Allen.

"I guess you know how much I thank you, Jim," she said. "I'm goin' to ride my present home."

"Shucks, 'taint nothin'," he mumbled, reddening. Then he added quickly: "Which way you ridin', Snippets? You ain't goin' through Dry Wash ?"

"No, I'm going the short way," she told him. Then she said with assumed carelessness: "So long. See you soon."

"Yeah," he replied tonelessly.

Allen stood motionless on the porch watching until the slender figure was no more than a dot in the distance. Finally even that disappeared. Allen's shoulders slumped; he seemed to grow smaller than ever. His face was haggard and lines crept out about his mouth. Then he turned and walked away.

Half an hour later Toothpick went out to search for Allen, but could not find him. He returned to the porch and gave himself over to meditation and sympathy for his friend. He was still sitting there when a riderless horse cantered across the clearing and headed toward the ranch house.

"Hell and damnation, there's the grey colt back!" Toothpick gasped, as he sprang to his feet.

He cleared the porch with one leap and shouted: "Hit it up! Come here, you colt!"

He sprinted to meet the grey, seized the reins; then he gave a strangled cry as he saw the dark stains on its saddle and grey coat. The colt itself was unwounded, but those stains were blood. Toothpick sprang into the saddle, swung the grey and brought his spurs home. The colt leaped forward like a rocket. She flashed across the clearing and tore down the trail toward Dry Wash.

Toothpick marked where her tracks before had left the main road and cut into the trail. Fast as the colt went, her rider still urged her to greater speed.

But when she struck the uneven, treacherous ground in Dry Wash, Toothpick made an effort to check her. The footing was uncertain, the curves abrupt; with every yard the colt risked a broken leg and he a broken neck. But those greys of Allen's had been trained to the sure-footedness of mountain goats. Not once did the colt make a mis-step, nor did she falter in her headlong course. She seemed to know the need for speed.

The colt swung down a steep slope which led to a stagnant pool of water. Toothpick's curses strangled in his throat. Before him lay three black dots on the white-clay soil — a horse, a man and —

The blood surged from Toothpick's face. All of those forms lay so still. He sprang from the saddle and stumbled toward Snippets. She lay in a crumpled heap, face down. Toothpick bent over her; at that first glance she seemed to be dead. He sprang to his feet, gun in hand, and dashed about through the surrounding rocks howling curses like a madman. But the murderers had long since fled; reason returned to him. He went back to the bodies.

The cow-puncher was certainly dead, but Toothpick raised Snippets' hand and felt the faint flutter of her pulse. He lifted the limp body and, holding it in his arms, managed to scramble back into the saddle.

Instinctively he started for the Bar II Bar, for that was nearer. He put the colt into a smooth gallop, climbed out of the wash across the level, and forded Muddy Creek. Nothing seemed real to him; he rode in a nightmare. Later he could remember only the sound of his own voice cursing and threatening the men who had done this thing.

Later he realized how it must have happened. They had been waiting for Allen. Snippets was about Allen's size and she was mounted on a grey horse.

As Toothpick neared the ranch house, he shouted. People came out of the door. Then, through a haze, Toothpick saw that another man rode beside him. The man's face was so pale, so strained, that he did not recognize him at first. And never once did Jim Allen look at Toothpick; his eyes were fixed on the still, white-faced figure in the puncher's arms.

Toothpick eased up before the house, and a big, red-haired man reached up and took his burden. Mac MacPherson was a slow-moving, slow-thinking man, but he acted quickly this day. A bellowed command, and a rider shot away from the ranch house and raced toward town for the doctor. Another shout, and women scurried to prepare hot water and bandages.

The Bar II Bar riders shouted questions at Toothpick. When they heard the story they milled about cursing monotonously. Then, with one accord, they raced toward the bunk house, to reappear with saddles and rifles. They besieged the cookhouse for provisions for a long chase; they rushed to tear open boxes of cartridges and fill the loops in their belts.

Jim Allen stood in a corner of the living room and stared at the door of the room where Snippets lay. Ma MacPherson appeared in the door; her face was swollen from weeping. She crossed to Allen and laid her hand on his arm; womanlike, she understood his sorrow, that he was a companion in her grief. Allen's eyes were fixed, staring. He did not seem to see her. He brushed his hands across his face.

"She said she was taking the short way," he said in a dull, flat tone. "I'd have warned her —"

Then slowly he straightened up; flecks of yellow flame shot through his eyes. His lips moved, but no words came. He licked them with his tongue and tried again.

"My guns." The words were nothing but a whisper.

The woman shrank away from him as he walked slowly toward the open door. The two women beside the bed turned and whispered to him to leave. One of them raised her voice and repeated her command sharply. Ignoring her, Allen walked to the bed and looked down at Snippets.

He stood there for several minutes. Neither of the women spoke to him again; they dared not.

At last he turned and looked about the room. Against the wall, hung on some pegs, were twin, black-butted Colts in worn holsters and supported by worn belts. Allen crossed the room and silently took them down. One by one, he slung the belts about his waist, patted the holsters until they fitted snugly against his thigh, then fastened them there with strips of rawhide.

As he crossed to the door he did not glance again toward the bed. It was as though he had taken his last good-bye a moment before.

In the outer room he found Toothpick and Mac MacPherson with two other riders. Toothpick started when he saw the guns; he opened his mouth to speak, but he glimpsed Allen's face and remained silent.

Allen passed them without a word, whistled for Princess, swung into the saddle and headed toward Dry Wash.

That night the word spread to Beaverville. It leaped to the German settlements. It flashed to the various ranches and across the valley to Land's End.

The Wolf had come back and was to ride the blood trail.

CHAPTER
EIGHT

The Black Hawks Meet

Men wondered why Mike, the bald-headed bartender of the Lone Star, was so genial that night. The house bought most of the drinks served over the bar. A tall puncher sauntered into the bar and called to Mike.

"You hear the Wolf has took the trail?"

"Sure; have a drink on the house," Mike replied cheerfully.

Hours slipped by; men's tongues were loosened by Mike's liberality. For the first time in months they talked openly of the Black Hawks.

The lights were going out in town; one by one the saloons were closing when men, alone and in groups of twos and threes, rode silently from all points of the compass toward an old barn on the outskirts.

Here they dismounted, whispered to a sentry, and entered the barn. All wore black slips over their heads with holes cut for the eyes and mouth, and black robes that resembled night-gowns. They ranged themselves at one end of the barn until more than a score were assembled. No one spoke. From afar off came the hoofbeats of a hard-ridden horse. These came nearer and nearer, then ceased suddenly. A man who wore a hood but no gown flung open the door and entered.

Someone called the meeting to order. Then the men in muffled voices began to make their reports. One reported the burning of a barn, another the leaving of a threatening letter. Five told of having horsewhipped a man.

"We report the burnin' of the Reiker barns an' stables," the leader of a small group said.

"An' I reports the Wolf is no more. We did as we were ordered," the man without the gown cried out suddenly.

"You sure? 'Cause I hears it was a gal by mistake an' the Wolf's on the blood trail!" piped up an excited voice.

"Silence!" commanded the man who had called the meeting to order. "You say you are sure you got the Wolf?"

"Damned sure!" said the man without the gown, positively.

A ripple of excitement sounded.

"Good," said the chairman. "We had heard a contrary rumour."

Several of the hooded men moved uneasily. They did not take kindly to murder. They felt that they were carrying things with too high a hand, but none there dared voice these thoughts.

The chairman held up his hand for order.

"Some here hesitate to take life. But when it is necessary —"

His voice trailed off in a choked and startled silence and he stared at the door. Then, as if he could not believe his sight, he raised his hand and straightened his hood so that the slits were directly opposite his eyes. One by one, the others followed his gaze; then they, too, stood in frozen silence.

There, with his back to the door, stood a hard-faced youth, watching the room with slit eyes that flamed yellow. He stood easily, his body swinging from side to side; and in each hand he held a big Colt. To the hooded men the gaping muzzles of those guns seemed as large as cannons.

"Gents, reach for the sky," said Allen softly.

Slowly the men raised their hands above their heads — every man there save the man who wore no gown. That man whirled and ducked; and his hand streaked down to his gun. There came a smashing double report. The man sprawled backward over a table. His gun dropped from his hand, his arms swung like pendulums for a minute, and then were still.

"Who's next?" called Allen. He crouched to peer through the smoke. His voice held a note of suppressed eagerness, as though he yearned for another to make a break.

The line rustled and shrank closer to the barn wall. The yellow eyes flashed back and forth along the line of silent figures. All shuddered with the conviction that he longed to send more of them after the man sprawled across the table.

"Who is he?" snapped Allen.

"Sam Speil," a quavering voice replied.

Both guns jerked toward the speaker. Allen had found the one he sought; a man whose fear would make him obey every command.

"Yank off that hood and let me look at you," he ordered.

The other raised trembling fingers to his hood and displayed a thin, white face topped with a thatch of black hair.

"What's your name?" The question came like the snap of a whip.

"Amos White," the other faltered. "What you goin' to do to us?"

"I don't know yet. I got a list of six names. If any of them six is here, I aim to send him to hell after Sam Speil. The rest of you — I'll draw your fangs. Then I don't know — unless somebody makes a break."

The very impersonality of Allen's voice carried conviction. Again the prisoners shuddered and reached higher. Their faces paled beneath their hoods in proportion to their guilty consciences.

"Come here, Amos White."

The dehooded man walked forward, trembling. Allen relieved him of his gun deftly and quickly; then he patted him for other arms. The gun he tossed into a far corner.

"Now the first man on the left come forward. You, Amos White, take his gun. If I find as much as a jackknife on him afterward, I'll blow you in two."

The man marched forward, his hands held high. His gun was removed and tossed into the corner. A

73

jackknife followed. Then White turned and held up a pair of handcuffs.

"What shall I do with these?" he asked.

"Throw them — No, wait. Have you all got a pair of those?"

White nodded.

"Pile 'em on the table."

Allen leaned negligently against the wall while the disarming process went on. The hooded men received the impression that he was deliberately feigning carelessness in the hope that one of them would make a move. The truth was that Allen did not know what to do with these men. They deserved punishment of some kind, but they were fools rather than villains. He marked a pile of rusty chain in the corner, and this gave him his idea. Each man carried his own shackles; he grinned sardonically. Ridicule was what they deserved, and ridicule was what they would receive.

He ordered White to link one end of the chain through a cuff, then snap it about a man's neck. White leaped to obey. After that the men came forward one by one, were disarmed, and then linked by the neck to the chain.

As each man's hood was jerked off by White, Allen leaned forward and peered into the exposed face, asked the name sharply, then relaxed again. When at last all were shackled in a long line, he ordered them to file out of the door. The last two in line were forced to carry the dead man.

"I'm telling you I hope one of you will make a noise or holler for your friends," Allen said earnestly.

He halted them just outside the door and held up a lantern so that all could see a roan horse with two white feet.

"Whose horse is that?"

"Sam Speil's," several answered.

"Then I got the right man."

He marched them to the rear of the stable, where he produced a pair of horse clippers; then he forced White to run the clippers through each man's hair, including his own, from front to back. They protested and whimpered, but a prod from one of his guns brought the protests to a quick end.

A window in the barn shot up; a hostler thrust his head out and shouted:

"What's goin' on here?"

"Black Hawks! Close your window!" Allen ordered sharply.

The man's head vanished and the window slammed. Allen grinned mirthlessly. When all heads were clipped, he marched them into the street of the sleeping town and fastened the chain to posts on opposite sides of the street. Then, having scrawled something on a board, he swung to the back of the grey horse that had been following him like a dog and galloped out of town.

The east was grey when he left. The chained men did not have long to wait for witnesses to their humiliation. At dawn a man came out of a near-by house, yawned, and gaped at the miserable men strung across the street. Then he vanished into the house again, and his voice could be heard calling excitedly. Soon he reappeared, followed by three more men. The four

75

gaped at the clipped heads, the handcuffs about the necks, then read the writing on the board.

"Let us loose," pleaded one of the prisoners.

But the watchers were too busy calling others to view the strange spectacle. Soon the town sprang to life and a crowd gathered, grinning and poking gibes at the unfortunate men.

A window was raised, and a woman called shrilly: "Amos White, what have you done to your head? What do you mean by making a fool of yourself that way? Come in here at once. Do you hear me? Come in here!"

Amos White hung his head, and the crowd broke into roars of laughter as the woman continued to threaten dire punishment if he did not obey at once.

Mike pushed through the crowd and gazed in spell-bound delight at the strange spectacle. Then he glanced at the dead man and read the scrawled notice.

Black Hawks clipped by the Wolf. The one who frees them is a Black Hawk.

No audible sound came from Mike's lips, but his great body quivered with the force of gigantic amusement. Then he threw open the doors of his bar and beckoned one and all to have a drink on the house.

CHAPTER
NINE

The Wolf Goes Alone

A sullen and mutinous crowd of cowpunchers milled about the front door of the Bar II Bar ranch house that morning. Their boss, Mac MacPherson, had forbidden them definitely to ride the trail of vengeance. He was backed by Duff Dorwin, the sheriff, who had arrived at dawn.

"He ain't my boss an' I'm sure takin' the trail after them damn coyotes just as soon as the doc tells us the worst," Toothpick growled.

"Me, too. Just let me get my hands on 'em. I'll learn 'em," Big Tom cried.

A short, pudgy rider looked at the big man and laughed.

"The trouble is they won't let you get your hands on 'em. They'll blow you apart afore you get close."

"Let it be lead, then." Big Tom puffed out his huge chest.

The riders let the joke drop; they were far too serious and anxious even to kid the big man.

Down from Beaverville in the bright morning sunlight rolled a swiftly moving cloud of dust. The wind opened and closed it fitfully, revealing intermittent glimpses of Jim Allen and his grey mare. The sullen crowd regarded the fast-coming new arrival with envy.

"Here's a gent what you, Mac, an' the devil can't hold back from takin' the trail," Toothpick grunted to the sheriff.

Dorwin did not answer. His face was a mask. He turned suddenly as though to enter the house; then, as if realizing that flight would be useless, he waited. He knew that if Allen was after him he would follow him even to the bedside of Snippets and kill him there. Dorwin twitched his shoulder and shifted the concealed holster under his armpit toward the front. Then he stood there watching Allen approach.

Allen slid from the saddle before Princess had stopped moving. The grey was covered with sweat and dust; she bore the signs of a horse that had been ridden far and hard.

"How is she?" Allen asked flatly of Toothpick.

"We're waitin' for the doc to come out now," the puncher replied gruffly.

Allen nodded. His face was haggard from strain and streaked with dirt. He had had no sleep that night and had ridden many miles. When he spoke, his voice was calm, and there was nothing in his face to show the raging volcano of hate and blood-lust that burned within him. He was like a tired boy.

"There was six of 'em, five headed toward Land's End. T'other circled, then headed back to town." So far Allen had ignored both the big, red-headed ranch owner and the sheriff. Now he nodded to the former and addressed Duff Dorwin.

"Sheriff, a man's a damn fool to go dry gulchin' an' straddle a hoss with a broken calk on his front shoe. I lost that jasper. It was dark about five miles this side of Beaverville, an' while I was huntin' for his trail, a gent shoots by me, an' I look at his trail an' sure enough it was the gent I wanted — bein' obligin'. Reckon he must have stopped to get a feed at a friend's house."

Allen stopped and rolled a cigarette. The sheriff struggled between fear and curiosity for a moment. Then he asked:

"You was sayin' you picked up this gent's trail again?"

"Yeah, he led me to a meetin' of Black Hawks. Them gents is sure fools. The whole damn town know it was Snippets an' not me that got downed, an' here I finds 'em celebratin' the death of the Wolf." Allen laughed grimly.

"An' what happened to this stupid galoot what rode the hoss with the broken calk?"

"Him? He won't do it no more, unless he does it in hell." For an instant it looked as though Allen's restraint had broken, for he rapped out the last words with the snarl of a cougar. Then he mastered himself and addressed MacPherson. "Mac, I want you to give me —"

"I'm no hypocrite an' I'm not sayin' I like you any better now than I did before, but you can have anything I got," the big rancher interrupted sturdily. His dislike of Allen was well known; he considered the little gunman scarcely human.

"I don't give a damn whether you like me or not," Allen said wearily. It was plain that he was indifferent to all save the job before him. "My grey done close to eighty miles last night. I want a fresh hoss an' some grub."

"Get him that roan," Mac ordered a rider. "An' go have cookie make up a bag of provisions."

The men jumped to their errands like shots from a gun. Allen sagged against the railing of the veranda for a moment; then he straightened and asked if he could have some coffee at once. At a nod from Mac, he made for the bunk house.

Big Tom slipped from the crowd unobtrusively and followed him. By this time the big man was fully enlightened as to the freckle-faced boy's real identity and in suitable awe. He coughed nervously as he approached Allen, who was gulping down black coffee and munching a cold flapjack.

"Mr. Allen, take me with you," he pleaded earnestly.

Allen looked at the big, earnest face and shook his head.

"I know folks thinks I'm scared an' I guess I was born without much backbone, but I've known Snippets ever since she was knee-high to a grasshopper, an' no bunch of mangy yellow dogs is goin' to bushwhack her without me goin' after them," said Big Tom.

"I know, but it's a one-man job." There was pity in Allen's heart for the big man who was struggling so desperately with his fear.

Tom blinked, and his walrus moustache drooped. Then he sighed and straightened.

"Reckon I got to go alone, then."

Allen looked at him. If the fool did try it alone, he would certainly be killed. Then an idea came to him. Princess was played out momentarily, but he must have her in the long chase he saw ahead.

"Can you keep your mouth shut?" he demanded.

The other nodded eagerly.

"You know the country back of Land's End? Could you tell me a place in the Broken Rim country where I could meet you?"

Big Tom began to draw a map of the Broken Rim country on the table top. Allen saw that, even if he was without nerve, he was no greenhorn in knowledge of that wild country.

"You got Indian Head on your right, an' Disappearin' Creek comes down from the Saw Tooth. About ten miles from where the canyons fork, there's a red rock called Three Toes."

As Tom talked, he placed sugar bowls and salt cellars and wet his finger to outline streams and canyons. To a stranger his map would have been gibberish, but to Allen it was comprehensible.

"In behind Three Toes there's a little blind box canyon. Three pine trees block the entrance. It's damn near in the centre of the Broken Rim country, an' I'll meet you there."

"All right, old boy. You let that grey of mine rest until late this afternoon. Then you take her over to Hill's. To-morrow you start with her for your box canyon an' be there night after to-morrow. Wait there till I find you."

Big Tom's eyes shone and his chest swelled.

Allen found that Toothpick had changed the saddle from Princess to the roan. His provisions were on the saddle and all was ready for him to start. Toothpick and several of the Bar II Bar riders were also ready to go.

"You ain't goin' with me," he said.

Before Toothpick could answer, the front door opened, and the doctor stepped out on the porch. He glanced about at the tense faces of the riders. Then he cleared his throat.

"She was hit three times, but the only serious wound is one on the right chest. This was high up an' the bullet passed all the way through. I've stopped the internal bleeding. With her strong constitution, she has a bare chance," he said kindly. "It's not necessary for me to tell you that we want no noise about the ranch."

He re-entered the house. Simultaneously several riders turned to their saddled horses and started to swing into the saddles. They knew they would lose good positions by going after the outlaws, but they were none the less determined to go. Snippets was a favourite with all.

"This is my job — an' no gent is goin' to horn in," Allen said. His voice was like ice.

The riders turned and scowled at him, gave a rumble of protest. Allen's yellow eyes flicked over them.

"Gents, those mangy dogs got Snippets, thinkin' her me. That makes it my job, an' any man who gets between me an' them or goes gallivantin' around mussin' up their trail, I'll kill."

The faces flushed angrily.

"Looka here, Jim. The sheriff just made me a special deputy, so I could get them coyotes legal," Toothpick cried, displaying his nickel badge.

"There ain't goin' to be no prisoners took," said Allen flatly. "So I don't want you an' your tin badge with me."

"Then I'll take it off." Toothpick unpinned the badge and handed it to the sheriff.

"Look here, Allen, you got to remember I'm the law an' you ain't got no —" the sheriff commenced. Allen silenced him with a sentence.

"Don't you figure them coyotes need killin'?"

The sheriff gave a quick glance about the circle of hard, grim faces and made up his mind. Better to sacrifice Curly Cole and the others than to arouse these men.

"Yeah, sure they does," he agreed.

"That's all right, then. 'Cause that's what they're gettin'." Allen turned to the group of scowling riders. "You boys want them coyotes got. Then I'm tellin' you to let me do it alone. I may follow 'em to hell, but I'll get 'em. An' I'll get 'em sure if I goes alone. If you go leavin' trails all over the damn country, I ain't so sure. There's five of 'em out there. I knows them all an' I promise to get 'em all."

He chuckled, and the sound sent a cold shiver up the spines of the crowd. Good as they were, trackers and fighters, they were glad that this yellow-eyed fury was not on their trail. They knew he would keep his word; they knew he would do it better alone than if they went with him. Regretfully they gave way and agreed to

83

remain at the ranch. Toothpick alone reserved his determination to be in at the death. He knew that if he could pick Allen up over in the Broken Rim country the little outlaw would be forced to take him along.

The punchers watched Allen ride down the lane and swing his roan into the Land's End trail. He rode slowly without any sign of haste or excitement. But there was an infinite and horrible menace in his slow, deliberate progress. He moved like Fate itself.

CHAPTER
TEN

Land's End

Allen had never been in the Broken Rim country before, but he had little difficulty in finding his way through the jumbled mass of canyons, mountains, and bare plains, for Big Tom had known his job and marked the identifying features of the landscape with skill.

Night had long since fallen when he drew up before the three trees that marked the entrance to the box canyon. Inherent caution made him dismount, tie his horse off the trail and enter the canyon on foot. He climbed the short slope and halted. There, not three hundred yards away, he saw a large camp fire.

Allen strode forward briskly. He would teach Big Tom a lesson. It was folly to light so large a fire. But as he neared it he stopped abruptly. That fire was too large for even Big Tom to build. Allen made a careful detour about it, then crept toward it again. At last he could see a bulky object at the side of the fire. He watched closely until he saw it move. That was no dummy figure. It was Big Tom right enough. But still he waited. Allen had learned patience; one mistake meant he might never live to make another.

He studied that figure. The blankets were drawn over Big Tom's head and seemed to be tucked in. To cover one's head was natural, but not to tuck the blanket in so tightly. There was something wrong in that.

Allen sat down to wait — wait until some sound told him he could advance or go for his gun. Time slipped by without a sound. Still he sensed that something was wrong. He waited until at last Warty Bill's patience gave out and he arose from his place of concealment and went to the fire.

Warty Bill grinned maliciously as he kicked the bundle, and groans issued from it. Then he reached down and yanked the covering from Big Tom's head. Allen saw that the big man was bound and gagged.

"The Wolf didn't show," said Warty Bill. "I'm askin' you some questions an' takin' your gag out, but I'm warning you, if you let out a howl, I'll cut you up in steaks."

He removed the gag, and Big Tom worked his lacerated jaws.

"I knows damn well the Wolf is comin' here, 'cause that damned old grey crow bait of hisn is here," the outlaw continued. "There ain't no use your lyin' to me. Spit it out. When's he comin'? Hustle or I'll carve you." He whipped a knife from his belt.

Big Tom's face was ashen; his eyes popped from his head as they fixed on the shining steel so close to his throat. He shuddered as the knife pricked his neck.

"You goin' to speak?"

"I tol' you Allen is dead, so how can he come? I stole his horse 'cause I wanted to avenge him an' I thought it proper to ride his horse." Big Tom's teeth were chattering so that his words were hardly intelligible.

"You big hunk of a yellow, shiverin', cowardly cur! You thought you could catch Warty Bill?" The outlaw kicked the prone figure.

"'Lo, Warty," called a voice.

Warty Bill swung about, and his hand dropped to the butt of his gun, but he did not draw it. He stood there staring incredulously at Allen, who was now on the farther side of the fire. Then he sucked in his breath, and the blood pounded up to his head. He crouched and balanced on the balls of his feet, but he marked the look of contempt on Allen's face. The little man had not even drawn a gun when Warty placed his hand on the butt of his. Allen stood there lightly, his body swaying, his hands limply at his sides.

"Heard tell you call Big Tom a cowardly cur. Anyway, he had the guts to lie to save a friend, an' he risked gettin' carved for it, too. Let's see how your nerve is. You can shoot a gal off a horse. You got guts to draw your steel?"

Death was at Warty's elbow, and he knew it. His face was pale and strained.

"Listen, Allen, you let me tell you about the sheriff. I'll spill the whole thing to you. He's the leader of the Black Hawks. His real name is Sam Lark!"

Warty poured out his words, talking against time. He was willing to betray a friend if that would save him, but he had no assurance that it would. As he talked he watched for some sign of inattention on Allen's part, anything that would give him the start of the draw.

"Where's the loot of the last robbery?" Allen snapped.

"It's where I put it under the floor in the sheriff's sitting room."

"So it was you who dug it up and double-crossed the others?"

"Sure it was me an' Kid Moore. That's why the sheriff went away so the gang wouldn't suspect him," Warty said eagerly.

"Who done the plannin' to bushwhack me?"

"The sheriff an' Curly that day you took us to jail."

Allen's attention seemed to wander for a second, and Warty ducked sideways and snatched out his gun. There came the crash of a double report. The fire flared upward in a shower of sparks from the impact of Warty's bullet. Warty himself stood on tiptoe like a diver, then he fell straight forward on his face.

Allen seized his legs and dragged him from the fire; then he turned to Big Tom.

The big man related his experiences excitedly while they were riding out of the canyon. He had reached the appointed meeting place on time and settled down to wait; but Warty had surprised him and taken him prisoner. He bewailed his hard luck.

"Seems like they always play me for a fool," he said miserably.

"You sure showed nerve when you refused to tell that hombre when I was comin'," Allen said kindly. "An' you sure took good care of Princess."

He was riding the grey horse and leading the roan.

"Where we goin' now?" asked Big Tom.

Allen smiled to himself at the proud emphasis the big man put on that word "we." Big Tom had once more recovered his assurance.

"Well, I figure it this way. We got the whole gang except Al Conners an' Curly Cole. I figger maybe they'll be shy of provisions by this time an' head for Land's End to get more," Allen told him. "Anyway, we may be able to pick up some news of them there. If we don't we'll head back into the Broken Rim country and hunt until we find them."

They reached Land's End after dark.

Land's End was a tough place, and its citizens didn't care who knew it. The Broken Rim country bordered it, and the Broken Rim had been a haunt and refuge for wanted men since the West was first settled. Hence most of the visitors to Land's End were those who slipped out of hiding long enough to buy provisions or indulge in a debauch. Here, too, the outlaws could gamble away or trade stolen loot. It was an uninviting place. The shacks and saloons and stores had never known paint. It was rough, it was crude, it was dirty; but it was heaven to a man who had been hiding in the lonely hills.

Allen and Big Tom dismounted outside the town and left their horses hidden in a thicket. Then they entered on foot. Allen racked his mind for a way to get rid of the man without hurting his feelings. At last an idea came to him. He led the way to the rear of the largest saloon and whispered:

"I'm goin' in at that door. You stand to one side an' keep guard."

Big Tom grinned with pride; he drew his big Colt and took his appointed position. Allen peered through the dirty window panes and saw a rough bar with six or seven men lined up before it. Nearer to him, at the rear, a few more played cards. Suddenly Allen started and swore softly to himself. He had seen the profile of one of the men at the end of the bar. It was Toothpick.

Then Allen saw something else — something which made him spring toward the rear door, yank it open, and jump inside. Two men who had come from a back room were creeping toward the unsuspecting Toothpick.

At the sound of the opening door they flicked their heads around and saw Allen. One of them was Curly Cole. Instantly he leaped backward and slammed the door behind him.

The other, Al Conners, finding his escape blocked, took three steps and leaped headfirst from the window.

He took sash and glass with him. Allen fired as he leaped; the two bullets caught him in mid-air. He left the floor a live man; he landed on the ground outside a dead one. From without came the bang of a heavy Colt.

"I got him, Jim!" roared Big Tom.

Toothpick stared in amazement. Allen, a gun in each hand, was covering the rest of the men in the room. They were sitting and standing, but in all cases their hands were held in conspicuous positions. A whisper had crept through the room, and there were none there who wished to try conclusions with the Wolf.

Allen looked at Toothpick with disgust.

"You damn fool, where did you come from?"

"Who, me? Oh, I just drifted up here to get a drink," said Toothpick easily.

"Well, ain't you got sense enough to watch your own back in a place what is filled with mangy coyotes?" Allen indicated the other patrons with a general sweep of his guns.

Toothpick grew sober.

"What you talkin' about?"

"Curly an' Al Conners was sneakin' up behind you while that bartender tol' you stories. Come on, let's get out of this." The two backed to the door. As they reached it, Allen added, partly to enrage Toothpick and partly because he liked Big Tom: "I'm betting we find Al Conners dead in the alley. I left Big Tom on guard there, an' I heard him shoot."

A very crestfallen Toothpick stepped out into the alley and saw Big Tom standing over the dead body of Al Conners.

"I got him, Jim. Nailed him as he comes through the window. Pretty a shot as you ever see," boasted Big Tom.

"Reckon I owe you my life again, Jim," Toothpick reflected.

"Give me the makin's an' we're even," Allen retorted.

"Shucks, make him give you the whole package," snorted Big Tom.

Toothpick, for once in his life, was too abashed to make a retort. They secured their horses, fed and stabled them, then found a room in a small hotel.

"To-morrow you two start back to old man Hill's place," Allen told them crisply. "Tell him they're all got except Curly, an' I'm startin' after him. In three days at noon I'll meet Hill in Mike's place. That's all now. I'm goin' to bed."

The next morning Toothpick and Big Tom rode disconsolately back to Pleasant Valley, while Allen plunged back into the Broken Rim country. By noon he had picked up the trail of the fleeing Curly again. This time he played no waiting game; he had Princess under him and she made no mis-steps even on the roughest ground.

For two days Curly turned and twisted, tried all the tricks that were in his bag. But the end was inevitable and sure. It came when Allen cornered him in a blind canyon. Little by little the Wolf had worn the quarry down until Curly made the one final mistake.

He trapped himself in a canyon of sheer walls from which there was no escape. There he snarled, a beast at bay. He fought with the cunning and savagery of despair. But it was over quickly.

When Allen rode away, Curly's black eyes stared sightless at the sky.

CHAPTER
ELEVEN

Under Orders

On the morning after Allen had written finis to the tragedy of the Broken Rim country, he turned the weary Princess into the long lane of the Bar II Bar Ranch. A shout greeted him as he pulled up before the house.

"Here's the Wolf back!"

Men ran from the corral at a stumbling gait in their high-heeled boots. Others poured from the bunk house and clustered about him, besieging him with questions.

"Where are they?"

"Did you get them coyotes?"

But Allen was silent, looking around the circle. At last someone understood the question in his eyes, though he could not force himself to ask it.

"She's doin' fine," said a gruff puncher. "She's still a sick girl, but the doc says she'll pull through."

Allen straightened in the saddle. The weary mask dropped from his face and he grinned down at them. He slipped from his saddle, then jerked a thumb toward the Broken Rim country.

"They're all over there."

"You didn't get 'em!" exclaimed someone in dismay.

93

"Shut your trap, you idiot! He means they're there permanent," another rider corrected grimly.

Ma MacPherson beckoned to Allen from the door. As he walked toward her, he heard her call back over her shoulder to someone inside.

"Maybe he ain't human, but Snippets wants to see him an' doc told me to let her. So you keep quiet."

Allen knew to whom she was talking and sighed. It didn't matter really whether or not the big Scotchman, Snippets' father, liked him, but he wished he did.

Mrs. MacPherson put both hands on his shoulders and looked into Allen's face; it was haggard and wan and tired. His eyes were dull brown; the yellow flecks had gone from them; and his cheeks were sunken so that even his pug nose and freckles could not make him seem boyish to-day.

"You poor boy, you look all done up," she said kindly, patting his shoulder. "Snippets wants to see you."

Allen followed her across the living room and into Snippets' room. A faint glow of colour rose in the girl's pale cheeks when she saw him. He stood looking down at her.

"Snippets, I hadn't ought to let you go alone that day," he said gravely.

She patted his hand and smiled faintly.

"It was my fault. You said not to go that way. But I wanted to see the colt work on the rough."

After that they sat in silence for a long time. Then suddenly her eyes fell on his guns and widened. Allen answered her unspoken words.

94

"I thought you was dead," he said simply.

Then he told her the story of the Black Hawks. When he had finished, she whispered: "You got to go on now, Jim. You can't stop. Think of the misery you'll save the women and children. You got to clean 'em out."

"But the law will be against me."

"You can't stop. Things will be all right later."

Half an hour afterward Princess went travelling toward town. Allen made as fast time as possible, but he was late for his appointment with Hill. He wondered idly what caused the rush to town that day. Every hitching post was filled with buckboards and saddled ponies. The whole county seemed to have turned out. Maybe there was a fair in town.

Allen slid from the saddle before the Lone Star Hotel and stood glancing about for a minute; then he entered the saloon. Here he found Toothpick and Hill awaiting him impatiently.

"Jim, I was afraid you wasn't comin'!" the old man cried.

"That damn coyote is up to somethin'," fumed Toothpick.

Allen grinned at Mike, who smiled ruefully in reply.

"It's this way, Jim. Our much-beloved sheriff has called a meeting of the whole damned town. He calls it the law-and-order meeting. I hear he's goin' to suggest that every man who ever was an outlaw, or suspicioned of bein' wanted elsewhere, or can't give a good account of hisself, be run right out of the county. He's smooth, an' if he plants the idea in them fools' heads that he is doin' good, there ain't nothin' we can do to get the idea out again. They won't believe a thing we say."

"Did you send that wire to my brother Jack?" Allen asked Hill.

"Yeah, an' gets back word nobody knows where Jack is," the rancher replied dejectedly.

"That damn skunk, Bill Reiker, has been got at," Toothpick added wrathfully. "He swears now he warn't kidnapped, but went willin', an' he swears it was us had the Black Hawk gowns on an' not them coyotes."

"We got to break up that meetin'," growled Hill.

"Yeah, but how?" asked Mike.

"Bluff!" Allen told him tersely.

Then he told them what Warty Bill had said. He instructed them to search for the loot in the place Warty had mentioned, beneath the sheriff's living-room floor. If they found it, they were to signal to him. If not, he would try his bluff.

"If Sam Lark is the sheriff's real name, he'll damn quick draw to stop my talkin'," Allen said quietly. "An' if he does, your meetin' is broke up."

"But he's a sheriff, after all. You'll be outlawed in this whole State again," Hill protested.

Allen shrugged, but his eyes shone.

"I'm actin' under orders."

Hill and Toothpick rushed out to collect a reputable group of witnesses to be on hand in case they found the loot. Allen waited a few minutes, then nodded to Mike and sauntered into the street.

Old Lady Reiker hailed him from the general store.

"So you're back, Jim? Now you tell me where you ran away to." She threw up her hands in horror when she caught sight of his guns. "You bad boy! What do you mean by wearing those things? You go right in there and take them off."

Allen laughed and tried to hurry on, but she detained him with one small hand on his arm.

"Whatever did you do to Big Tom? He's so stuck up there's no living with him. He claims he helped you clean out a band of the most terrible bad men. And he says he killed one himself."

"He did, I guess," said Allen solemnly. "Big Tom was sure a regular hero."

"I always knowed it!" cried the old lady delightedly.

At last she released him, and Allen hurried to the town hall and slipped inside. It was packed with men and a sprinkling of women. Little by little, he squirmed his way through the press until he was close to the speaker's platform. Four men sat there. The speaker, a genial man with a sonorous voice; Kid Moore; the sheriff, and a man Allen did not know.

"Now ladies — for I see there are a few here — and gents, I'm goin' to stop this harangue an' introduce you to your popular young sheriff," the speaker ended, turning to Dorwin. "Gents and ladies — Duff Dorwin, your sheriff."

Men in different parts of the house commenced to clap and cheer. Allen grinned as he realized that Dorwin had packed the house with his friends to start a demonstration. Slowly the rest of the crowd took up the clapping. At last the whole house cheered. Again and again Duff Dorwin held up his hand for silence, but the crowd cheered for several minutes before he could speak.

"Ladies and gentlemen, I have called this meeting to see if there is not something we can do to put an end to the lawlessness in this valley," he said. "The other night some one started to expose and ridicule the Black Hawks. I don't know for certain who put that placard near them after they were clipped and harmless. Whoever did it probably had a good sense of humour, for while I desire to accuse no one, it has been reported to me that the one who was supposed to have signed that placard is himself a member of that wretched band."

At this a storm of hisses broke from some punchers who were Allen's friends and a stentorian voice shouted:

"That's a lie!"

The uproar went on for a minute, then the sheriff obtained silence.

"Gentlemen, remember I am not saying he was a member of that society. But Bill Reiker says he is. You remember Allen arrested Curly Cole and four others and accused them of kidnapping Bill Reiker. I was forced to lock them up. Later that night they escaped and fled to the hills. It was not my fault they escaped and I am sorry they did, for they were innocent.

"Bill Reiker swears he went with them willingly, that Allen and his friends were dressed as Black Hawks when they burst in the house." The turmoil began to break out again, and the sheriff shouted hastily: "Bill Reiker, stand up, and tell them the truth."

Bill Reiker called quickly: "Sure, that's the truth."

Even Allen's friends were puzzled at this, but not Big Tom. He arose from his position in the front row and roared:

"You're a damn liar. You tol' me yourself that Curly was all set —"

Here the sheriff's friends interrupted with an uproar that drowned out the rest of Big Tom's words.

"Shut up!"

"Throw him out!"

Some one pulled the big fellow back into his chair, and the sheriff continued. Very cleverly, without definitely saying so, he managed to give the impression that he himself had captured and clipped the Black Hawks. Again and again Allen looked toward the door.

At last he saw Hill crowd in and give him the agreed signal. They had not found the loot. Well, that meant he had to bluff.

"What I'm going to ask you to do is to give me power to run out of this county all questionable characters." The sheriff came to a climax. "All those who have been outlaws, those who are suspected, those —"

"Aw, shut up!"

Allen leaped upon the platform and stepped toward the sheriff. He saw Kid Moore jump to his feet and stand beside Dorwin.

"Gents, ladies and the sheriff — let me talk as one of them who is goin' to be run out of the county. 'Cause I was sure an outlaw once." He grinned at the audience, and there were many there besides his friends who smiled in return at that loose, lovable grin.

"Look here —" began the sheriff.

Allen whirled on him.

"Are you an' your friends scared to let me talk?"

Dorwin's self-control was supreme. He smiled good-naturedly.

"Certainly we should hear from the other side," he said affably. "I won't say from the bad element, but from those who are to be run out of the county."

"All right, gents. I'm the bad element. In the first place, those what knows Bill Reiker knows he's a liar. The sheriff says Curly an' his bunch got out of jail by themselves. Then I'm askin' you how they got their guns an' rifles out of the sheriff's office? They were over in the Broken Rim country with their own guns, their own rifles, their own saddles an' hosses." He swung about and faced the sheriff. "How come, sheriff?"

"You can't prove it," Dorwin said quickly.

Allen tossed a burlap bag on the floor at his feet.

"Their guns are in there, an' they was marked by Mr. Hill, afore you put them in your safe, by my request."

The sheriff glanced about the hall, trying vainly to signal his friends to create a disturbance and divert the crowd's attention.

"You say outlaws are to be barred? Good!" Allen paused, he swayed back and forth, his hands close to his guns. "Then if Jim-twin Allen goes, does Sam Lark also go?"

The sheriff winced as if he had received a blow. So Allen knew that. The time for words had passed. He must never be allowed to make that direct accusation. Dorwin slumped low and Kid Moore, behind him, fell into a half crouch.

A tense silence fell. Few of the people in the audience understood the significance of Allen's words, but all could see the drama. Then the silence was broken by the stentorian voice of Big Tom.

"I got him, Jim. He was tryin' to pot you in the back."

Allen dared not look at the enemy, a friend of Dorwin's, whom Big Tom held pinioned.

"All right, Mr. Sheriff — Mr. Duff Dorwin — Mr. Sam —"

As a snake strikes, the sheriff's left hand shot inside his coat and appeared with a shining gun. Kid Moore's hands were a blur as they flashed to his weapons.

Then five heavy Colts roared together so closely that their clatter blended into one great wave of sound; it beat against the spectators like volleys of thunder.

The sheriff's gun blazed once only. Bill Reiker, who was close to the platform, screamed and fell forward. Then the sheriff gave a little jump, plunged off the platform and landed with a crash at the feet of the spectators.

Kid Moore's right-hand gun was a fraction faster than his left; his first shot from that hand tore a great gash along Allen's arm. But Kid Moore's other gun never came level. He fired twice more, but his bullets splintered into the floor. Allen worked both of his big

101

guns so fast that a continuous stream of fire and smoke poured from their muzzles. Moore was dead before he hit the floor.

Then there was silence.

For a moment the crowd was too petrified to move; then it surged forward with one accord.

"Get him!"

"Get the Wolf!"

"He killed the sheriff."

Allen leaped to a side window; he smashed out the glass with the Colts, then he leaped to the sill. For a moment the mob saw him framed there in the midst of swirling smoke. Then he was gone.

The men milled around, shouted threats and howled for vengeance. They poured into the street, but they found no sign of Allen. Both he and his grey had vanished.

When the people had cooled down, Hill and the others went about explaining. When the telegram finally came from Jack Allen with the description of Sam Lark, the townsmen admitted shamefacedly that they had been fools. The dead sheriff's friends packed their belongings and flitted away that night.

CHAPTER
TWELVE

Resting Up

"Slim" Dent dropped his saddle close to the corral fence and heaved his packed war bag on top of it. He rolled a cigarette, discontentedly, and stood glowering about him for a moment.

From the grub house, a hundred yards from the corral, there came the clatter of tin plates and cups, and the humming voices of a score of riders, busy with their morning chow. Slim listened, then threw his cigarette away and ground out the fire beneath a vicious heel. He yanked the rope from his saddle, opened the corral gate, and started toward the bunch of milling horses. Deftly he dropped his rope across a big bay gelding and led him outside to the saddle.

He had adjusted the bridle and was about to throw on the saddle, when he glimpsed two riders coming out of the grey dawn across the purple mesa toward the ranch. Both were riding grey horses. He squinted at them, dropped his saddle, and squatted on his heels close to the fence.

"Here comes the boss — might as well wait to say good-bye," he grumbled. "Time he was comin' home."

"Old Doc" Steward was a tall, gaunt man of fifty-five. He peered from beneath shaggy eyebrows at Slim Dent. A fleeting smile crossed his heavily lined face, as he asked:

"Yuh had a fight with Madge?"

Slim Dent glanced from Old Doc to the other rider, a stranger to him. This new man looked like a small, skinny youth, dressed in the tattered clothes of a scarecrow. Heavy bandages covered his head and concealed most of his face, revealing only a pair of brown eyes, a freckled pug nose, and part of a wide, loose mouth.

Slim moved uncomfortably. He did not relish discussing his affairs before a stranger.

"No, I haven't had a fight with her," he mumbled.

"Then why the packed war bag?" Old Doc insisted.

"Just restless, I guess."

Old Doc stepped down from his horse and, laying his hand on Slim's shoulder, said:

"Son, Madge is like a hoss with the bit between her teeth an' —"

The stranger grinned through his bandages and interrupted:

"Doc, yuh sure is correct. Women is like hosses — when they start runnin', yuh got to let 'em run until they gets tired before yuh starts to gentle 'em."

"Why you horning in?" Slim Dent glowered.

"Excuse me," the stranger said amiably. "I always did talk too much."

He rode off toward the ranch house, and Slim turned to Old Doc with a scowl.

104

"Who's that fresh kid?" he demanded.

"He's Jimmy — Ashton." Old Doc glanced shrewdly at Slim, to see if the latter had noted his hesitation before he spoke the last name. He saw that Slim Dent was too troubled with his own affairs to notice anything else.

"Son," Old Doc continued seriously, "Madge is sure goin' to need friends pronto, an' I reckon yuh're too much of a man to run away when she might need yuh."

Slim kicked at the dust with his spurred boot, stooped and picked up his saddle and war bag. Carrying them, he followed Old Doc toward the ranch house.

Old Doc led the stranger to a small shed at the rear of the barn and assisted him in the stabling of the two grey horses. Fifteen minutes later the two men entered the ranch house. Doc's faded-blue eyes lit with pleasure as they rested on the piquant face of Madge Finkle, his niece.

"Madge, meet Mr. Ashton." He waved toward the stranger. "We is plumb starved."

The girl nodded to Ashton and he grinned a reply. "Ma'am, those pancakes sure look good to a gent what is near hollow."

"Draw up a chair, stranger, and get busy, then," a young man of nineteen invited cordially.

"Jimmy, meet Steve. He's my nephew and Madge's tenderfoot brother." Old Doc chuckled.

"Tenderfoot, huh! Ain't I been in this country as long as Madge? She's the tenderfoot — not me — with

105

her fool notions about peace and the Golden Rule. People are laughing their heads off at her and stealing her cows right and left. It's too darned bad Uncle Frank didn't leave the ranch to me, instead of to her."

"Why?" Madge snapped.

"Because, if I owned the place, I'd treat 'Curly' Watson like Uncle Frank would have. I'd stick 'Red' Casey on him —"

"I'll 'tend to Curly Watson in my own way," Madge cried firmly, "and it will be just as effective as committing murder."

"Ask him politely to move off your range!" Steve snorted in disgust.

"Is Curly Watson a half-breed?" the stranger suddenly asked, after gulping a mouthful of pancakes.

Old Doc nodded. His eyes twinkled at the surprise he saw in Jimmy Ashton's face. Madge's mouth was drawn in a straight, thin line, and her brother, reading the danger signal, lapsed into silence.

Madge glanced up and greeted Slim Dent with a coldly polite nod when that young man entered the room. Her eyes were frosty as they rested on the low-hung holster and gun. Slim flushed uncomfortably, threw himself into a chair, and stared with sullen eyes at his boots.

A moment later Madge pushed back her chair, entered her office, and slammed the door.

Old Doc grunted and grinned cheerfully at Slim's miserable face. He carefully wiped his plate clean with a piece of bread; then he asked gravely:

"What riled her majesty?"

"Red Casey caught the Dawson brothers down near Bear Creek. They had a straight iron."

Old Doc nodded. He and the others knew, without being told, what had happened to the Dawson brothers.

"And she found out?"

"Yeh, some fool blabbed, and she's aiming to tell Casey a few things. Threatens to fire him — she gave the boys a talking to last night. That, with other things, was why I was aiming to quit," Slim explained.

The old man frowned, bit off a large piece of black plug and expertly kicked a sawdust-filled box into a more accessible angle. After a moment he said:

"Mister Ashton here don't savvy what this is about, so I'm goin' to elucidate. Jimmy, yuh knew the major, my brother."

Jimmy Ashton nodded: "And he was sure a fighting fool."

"Sooner fight than eat. Well, he stopped a slug a while ago and left this place to Madge. She comes out here and has a hell of a time playin' queen — gives orders and rides about — and says the law is here."

Jimmy Ashton grinned widely:

"She figgers that the law is come in this here country, where there ain't only a sheriff for every hundred miles? Well, she'll sure learn different."

"She is learnin' fast. Yuh see, she lives here on the Bar X, with me, and bosses her ranch, the Double X, which is about ten miles to the north from here."

"Yuh mean," Jimmy said shrewdly, "she thinks she bosses the Double X. From what I hears, Red Casey takes her orders and then does what he wants."

"Yeah," Old Doc grunted. "But she's discoverin' things, and I'm scared of ructions."

Steve broke in with a chuckle:

"She told her boys, now that justice had arrived on the range, there wasn't any need for them to pack guns and ordered them to go hang up their guns and forget them. Every time she goes over to the Double X, the boys has to hide their guns."

"What's the idea of keeping things from her?" Slim exclaimed in disgust.

"Don't do no harm," Doc said.

"It don't, eh? Hell, she won't have a cow left, soon. The Double X boys, even before she cut loose yesterday, was discouraged. If they get fired every time they gun a rustler, they won't be looking very hard. And Curly and that Frying Pan outfit are pushing our cows clean out to the Twin Creek country. Over a month ago, the day you left for the Sawteeth, they threw some cows in there, and waited around to see what would happen."

"What happened?" Doc asked.

"Red Casey sends a couple of men in there and drives them out. There's some shooting, and Madge hears of it and gives Red fits for telling his men to use their guns. Curly hears of this and runs back more cows and, as Red don't dare do nothing, because of Madge, he hogs the whole range. I tell you, Double X cows will be hungry this winter."

"That's bad." Old Doc became thoughtful.

"What's your idea of letting her ruin herself?" Slim demanded heatedly.

"She owns the Double X — not me!" Old Doc said bluntly. "I reasons with her at first, but —"

"You should of turned her over your knee and spanked her," Steve said, with brotherly directness.

"Jimmy here says women is like hosses. If they take the bit, you got to let them run afore yuh gentle them."

"Meaning yuh'll let her run until she's broke?"

"Exactly, and if she admits she's wrong then, why she's saved. Reckon her soul is worth a few cows."

Later that morning Old Doc and Jimmy Ashton were locked in the former's office.

"Now then, Jim, off with your coat and let me look at that arm," Old Doc said.

Jimmy Ashton obediently threw off his coat, and Old Doc grinned when he saw the two big pistols, strapped beneath the little man's arms. But he grew very serious and thoughtful after he had examined Jimmy's forearm. From wrist to elbow the arm was like that of a child. It was one big scar.

"Soft-nosed .45 slug," Jimmy explained.

"She'd sure dried up on yuh in another few weeks — but I guess I can fix her up," Old Doc stated. "Now, Jim, no one will know yuh, with those bandages I wrapped about your head. So you got to stay and let me fix her up. It'll hurt some, too."

As Doc worked on Allen's arm he marvelled at the little outlaw's fortitude. The arm upon which Old Doc worked was as limp as that of a dead man, and Allen's freckled face was as expressionless as if the doctor was manicuring his nails rather than cutting deep into his living flesh.

"Gosh, Jim, you're sure a marvel," Old Doc admired.

"Shucks, a gent gets used to standin' things," Allen replied simply.

"There, that's finished." Doc's relief was evident, then a little later he added gruffly: "I see you're packin' guns again."

"Yeah."

"I heard tell about that ruckus you had down Beaverville way. That where you got this slug?"

"Yeah, some one nailed me as I was goin' through the window of the courthouse," Allen explained.

"How's the gal Snippets?"

The moment Doc had his question out he regretted it, for Allen's face in a flash grew old, and those strange eyes of his clouded with pain.

"Dang it, Jim! Can't you slip out where no one will know you and take Snippets with you and marry her?" Doc said gruffly.

Allen was silent for a time and when he replied his voice was tired, like that of an old man.

"Shucks, Doc, I'm wanted dead or alive in every state in the West. There's nowhere I could go without some gent catchin' on. I could grow a beard, but I could never hide these eyes of mine. Nope, there ain't no place I could take Snippets except to the desert and make another Wolf of her."

Doc sighed and let the matter drop, for he knew that Jim Allen spoke the truth.

That afternoon Madge, who had been walking about the place trying to figure out some plan by which she

110

could save her range without resorting to bloodshed, surprised Jimmy feeding pieces of pie to his two greys.

The two greys were gaunt, ugly brutes, with small heads and wicked eyes. Madge watched the tattered little figure feed them, first with alarmed surprise, then with delight. For she soon realized that their vicious snapping of teeth was only in play. The three were playing a game. She then delighted Jimmy Ashton by insisting on joining the game and feeding them herself.

The girl divined that the horses were more to him than mere pets. They were friends — partners. After he had put them through several tricks, he blushed like a schoolboy at her praise.

"Why, they mind you just like two dogs," she cried.

By the time they returned to the ranch house they were firm friends, and Madge was laughing at an absurd story, told by him, about Mexican twip dogs.

"What a fibber you are!" she said gayly. "You couldn't possibly have been to all those places you tell about. You are too young."

Slim Dent saw them and scowled at Old Doc.

"Who's that kid?"

Old Doc chuckled.

"You jealous?"

Slim Dent swore.

CHAPTER
THIRTEEN

Jimmy Steps In

On the following morning Madge announced her intention of visiting Twin Creek and ordering Curly Watson off her range. When Old Doc and Slim Dent protested, she replied that Curly would listen to reason from a woman, while if she sent a man, there would be a fight. It was only when she said she was taking Jimmy Ashton with her that Old Doc ceased his protest. But not so Slim.

"Madge," Slim cried anxiously. "Curly's a half-breed, and you won't be safe. Let me, or some other man, go with you."

"No thanks," Madge replied coldly. "If I do, will you go unarmed?"

"To see that half-breed?" Slim stormed.

"That's it — you believe in fighting, in murder — I don't. Therefore I'm going with Jimmy."

Old Doc chuckled, but when he glimpsed Jimmy's miserable face, he brought his mirth to an abrupt halt. After the two had ridden off, Slim turned to Old Doc and cried angrily:

"What did you let her go alone with that little runt for?"

Old Doc ignored the question and chuckled.

"That's sure a joke — she wouldn't go with yuh, 'cause yuh killed a man in self-defence, and she goes off with Jimmy."

"I don't see anything funny in that," Slim fumed. "And she likes him."

"I hope she does. 'Cause, if she does, your hands is washed lily-white by comparison."

But in spite of Slim's questions, Doc refused to explain what he meant by this remark.

It was high noon when Madge and Jimmy Ashton topped the rise above Twin Creeks and headed down the farther side toward Curly Watson's camp. When the two rode up, Curly's hardbitten riders were eating their dinner. They greeted Madge with derisive smiles.

Curly Watson was a swarthy, heavy-set man of thirty. His thick lips parted in a leer as he spoke to the girl.

"Howdy, ma'am, come and eat grub with me?"

Madge shook her head and said coldly: "Mr. Watson, I have come to ask you to leave my range and —"

"Your range?" Curly interrupted. "Boys, she says this is her range. Ma'am, did you buy it from the government?"

Madge knew they were laughing at her, and her face flushed. But after an effort she regained her composure and said firmly:

"It belonged to my uncle, Major —"

Curly again interrupted: "This land belongs to the government, and I have as much right here as you, and I intend to stay — 'cause justice and peace has camped on this range."

At this shot Curly's men guffawed. Madge was staggered. She felt that Curly was telling the truth. She thought quickly and brought the ancient range law to her aid.

"Maybe you are telling the truth — but custom gave it to my uncle and therefore, as his heir, it is mine," she cried firmly.

"Custom?" Curly sneered. "Custom of discovery — huh, the major wasn't the first one here."

"I shall ask the sheriff to make you move away," Madge cried, as she and Jimmy rode away. They were followed by derisive shouts from Curly and his men.

"Sort o' hard to talk sensible with gents like Curly, ain't it?" Jimmy said thoughtfully.

Madge glanced sharply at him, but she could detect no guile in his face. They rode in silence for a moment, then Jimmy added: "I sort o' remember the major had a hot fight over the Twin Creek range. There was another gent here first, and the major ran him out."

"Oh!" breathed Madge. "Then I don't own it."

"Sure yuh do — 'cause the gent who the major run off chased another gent off before him. So that's all right, as neither of them was Curly."

"I will make the sheriff put Curly off, because I have to have this range for winter feed for my stock," Madge cried.

Jimmy grinned to himself. Madge was learning the first lesson of the range. Her uncle had learned it before her, and had fought to obtain it.

The Double X Ranch lay along the banks of Sandy Creek, some ten miles north of the Bar X. It ran ten times as many cattle as the Bar X, and, in the major's time, was always trying to add to its holdings.

Red Casey was a thoroughly efficient foreman. He had been the confidant and right-hand man of Major Steward and had accompanied that grim old warrior on many a raid, either in reprisal or as a warning not to crowd too closely. He admired the way in which the major had built up his vast holdings. One day, when they were new to the range, a cattleman, who was being crowded away from the Twin Creek country, threatened to appeal to the law. The major had bristled like a grizzly bear and thundered:

"Law! The law is the Colt, and you can draw it when you like."

Red was willing to serve Madge, as he had been her uncle; fight to keep what she now had, and if necessary to add to it. But when the new boss insisted that reprisals stop, that the Colt and force be laid away on the shelf, and that justice be given a chance, he had at first humoured her and pretended to do as she ordered. Then, when she continued on her mad course, he had grown sullen and watched with bewilderment the possessions left by the major start to melt. Red loved the Double X, as only a man could who had fought and bled for it.

Madge arrived at the Double X on the return from her trip to persuade Curly Watson to vacate the Twin Creek country. She dismounted before the broad verandah of the home ranch. She ordered a passing rider to inform Red Casey that she was awaiting him.

115

The rider passed to the rear of the house, crossed to the corral where Red was watching two punchers break horses, and said:

"Her high and mightiness wants yuh pronto."

Red swore, then sullenly walked toward the house. A puncher called after him:

"Hey, Red, I'm bettin' she'll make yuh do yuhr hair up in curl papers."

Several riders rocked with mirth at this rough jest. Red swore again. He knew he was losing prestige among the men. They were getting out of hand. They knew he did not dare boss them with a gun for fear of losing his job. He cursed beneath his breath — things had reached the breaking point. He would tell this fool girl a few things and then quit.

Dan Smith hobbled out of the kitchen to meet him. Dan had been crippled in one of the major's battles and now acted as cook.

"Red, don't yuh quit," he advised.

"I can't stand it no longer. Damn it, I love the Double X; I fought to make it. It sure hurts to see a fool girl let it go to smash," Red growled sullenly.

"All right — if she won't let yuh fight to keep it for her, then fight to keep it for yourself," Dan said.

Red Casey stared. Dan whispered to him for several seconds. At first Red listened with a frown, then his eyes flashed with the joy of coming battle.

"Hell!" he cried. "I'll do it and, when I get it, I'll keep it."

"Mr. Casey," Madge said, when her foreman stood before her. "I have had a talk with Curly Watson and have decided, since neither of us own the Twin Creek range, to share it with him."

"Suppose he drives our cows off — what then?" Red asked coolly.

Madge had expected opposition to her proposal and she grew suspicious of this cool acceptance of it. She looked sharply at Red, but he had a poker face. Absolutely expressionless grey eyes looked out from beneath his flaming-red hair. His smile, as he met her gaze, was quite unreadable.

"If he does, you hold the men at the ranch and tell me. I will hold you responsible. If there is a fight you will be out of a job," Madge said sharply.

Red grinned easily.

"What will yuh do?"

"I'll see the sheriff."

"He won't do nothin'," Red said bluntly. "He's afraid of Curly."

"If he doesn't, we'll get another sheriff."

Red laughed — laughed as one does at a child. Madge flushed with helpless rage and could think of nothing to say.

"You hold the men here — or look for another job," she repeated.

Red grunted and scratched his head, as Madge and Jimmy Ashton rode away.

"Women — hell — them that likes 'em can have 'em — give me a hoss and a gun," he said.

He aroused himself and started toward the chow house, and, as he went, his eyes glittered with the joy of the born fighter who scents a coming battle.

117

Slowly, without haste, he began to gather at the home ranch the best fighters among the Double X riders and he picked men who owed allegiance to none but himself.

Both Madge and Jimmy Ashton were silent on the return trip to the Bar X.

"Poor girl," Jimmy thought to himself. "She's all right, but she got started wrong — the jump from East to West was too sudden, and she's due to lose her ranch."

Days passed, and nothing happened. Curly waited; then, when no move was made to run him from the north side of Twin Creek, he threw a few cows over to the south bank. A few days later he threw more, then his whole herd.

Madge learned of his move and, accompanied only by her brother, Steve, she started for Benton, the country seat, to force the sheriff to help her make Curly reasonable.

About a half hour after Madge started to seek the aid of the sheriff, Red Casey, at the head of the hard-bitten riders, sallied forth to settle the affair in the major's way.

Madge's interview with the sheriff proved most unsatisfactory. The sheriff was an elderly, hard-working man who daily took his life in his hand, and when Madge accused him of being afraid of Curly, instead of throwing her out, as he would have if she had been a man, he only sighed and said patiently:

118

"Ma'am, Curly's got fifteen hellions, so maybe I is afraid of him. Yuh say yourself, yuh don't own that country, so I don't see what I can do. Yuh can't get the law to run a gent off government land when yuh don't own it."

Madge stormed and insisted that the sheriff help her, but the old man insisted he could do nothing.

Then Fate laughed and played a card.

Curly walked into the sheriff's office. His eyes were bloodshot, and his thick lips drawn back in a snarl.

"Howdy, Curly," the sheriff greeted. "Suppose you tell us what you know about the Twin Creek ructions."

The half-breed's small eyes flickered with rage as they rested on Madge's slim, imperious face.

"You been comin' to him with tales, while Red jumps my outfit and cleans up!" he cried furiously.

"What do you mean?" Desperately Madge attempted to control her voice and keep it cool. "I don't know what you are talking about. I especially ordered Mr. Casey to keep my men at home."

"And winked," Curly laughed coarsely. "You're a goody-goody, ain't you? Women — hell —"

As a foul epithet left Curly's lips, Steve Finkle promptly knocked him down. The sheriff saved the boy's life by kicking the gun from the half-stunned man's hand.

Slowly Curly arose to his feet, and Madge recoiled before the blood-lust she saw in his eyes. He wiped his bruised mouth and said thickly: "I'm warnin' you, Steve, I'll kill you the next time I see you."

It is probable that Madge discounted the threat against her brother's life, for it was certainly not fear that moved her to leave town immediately, but rather a furious desire to settle with Red Casey for breaking her orders.

She slurred over Curly's threat to Steve, when relating the affair to her uncle that night.

"What are you going to do?" Doc inquired.

"Discharge Casey," she said firmly. After a moment a frightened look came into her eyes.

"You don't think that man will really hurt Steve?"

"Curly's a killer." Old Doc spoke seriously.

"Then the sheriff must —"

"He can't do nothin' until Curly does somethin'." He waved his hand, and his face was hard, as he interrupted the girl. "Now, you listen. You've given us to understand that you don't want advice, and I ain't offering to give none about your cows. Go ahead and fire Red — if he'll fire — but we got to do somethin' about Curly or he'll kill Steve."

"Steve must stay close about the house," Madge faltered.

"He can't stay here for ever — something has got to be done. Steve can't throw a gun."

"Thank Heaven!" Madge cried fervently. "I suppose you mean by something being done — that someone will have to gun Curly."

Old Doc nodded.

Now if the truth was known, Madge was badly frightened, and the unpleasant thought had commenced to penetrate into her mind that her brother had been correct in his statement that everyone was laughing at her, that she was only a figurehead of a queen without power. As to that, she intended to show them. In her hurt pride she looked for some one upon whom to empty the vials of her wrath — and she found Slim Dent.

"Of course you would do it," she said.

Slim squirmed.

"Curly's bad — but —" Old Doc began.

Madge never considered that Slim's offer to attempt to eliminate Curly carried personal danger.

"But it wouldn't matter — his hands could be no redder," she said cuttingly.

Old Doc's bewilderment gave place to anger.

"You're a little fool," he said bluntly. "Maybe, after Curly kills Steve, you won't be so plumb righteous. Seems to me you're letting your principles play mighty loose with Steve's life. Slim was offering to take a big chance of getting killed himself, and you're actin' plumb as if he was offering to do something dishonourable. You're a little fool."

At this Madge tossed her head.

A little later, accompanied only by Jimmy Ashton, she started for the Double X Ranch. She was white with rage when at last she faced Red Casey. The foreman listened to her tirade without interruption, and when she finally finished from lack of breath, he said coolly:

"Ma'am, I helped the major make this place, I fought for it, and I ain't figurin' on lettin' no breed like Curly steal it, so me and the boys run him off. Yuh tell me I'm

121

fired. In that, yuh're makin' a mistake — 'cause when I saw yuh didn't care enough for the place to fight for it — I took it myself."

"You took it?"

"Yep — I took it and I'll keep it — from you an' everyone else."

"How dare you talk like that? Leave this ranch at once!" Madge stormed.

"Nothin' doin'. I own it. The major left me four-fifths of it," Red said coolly.

"That — that's a lie! He left me four-fifths and you one-fifth."

"Yuh got it mixed, ma'am; it was just the other way."

With great deliberation Red took from his pocket a folded paper and handed it to Madge. The girl opened it and, as she read it, her lips commenced to tremble and the colour left her face.

"It's — it's a forgery," she gasped.

"Maybe so, ma'am — but yuh got to prove it."

Red returned the paper to his pocket, swung on his heel, and clanked into the house. Madge stared after him, then mounted her horse and started back toward the Bar X. Her reason told her that the paper was a forgery. She was bewildered. She felt that public opinion would back Red in his move. She felt that there was little chance of the law returning the ranch to her. Into her numbed brain the realization came that she had acted the part of a fool. No one person is able to change the opinions of a whole State.

That night she went supperless to bed and was glad that Old Doc was not there to pester her with questions. The following morning it was a very pale and red-eyed girl who came to the breakfast table. She had thought it out and she was determined at all costs to prevent her friends from paying with their lives for her mistake. She would not permit them to fight Casey.

Doc and Slim Dent were still away. At the table she was confronted only with Jimmy Ashton. It was not until later that she thought to question the Chinese servant as to the reason of her brother's absence.

"Steve go town, bluy him a gun," he told her.

For a moment the full significance of this did not reach her brain, but when it did, it hit her with the force of an explosion. Steve in Bolton — to buy a gun. She shuddered as she remembered Curly's threat. What if the two met? Leaving word for her uncle to follow as soon as possible, she saddled her pony and galloped toward the town.

Madge had been gone for nearly an hour, before Jimmy Ashton learned of her departure. The tattered, bandaged little man wasted no time in words. He was speeding on the back of one of his greys toward Bolton five minutes after he heard the news.

The girl was in Bolton for fully half an hour before she discovered her brother. Then she met him in the open street, directly before the Bolton Hotel. He was wearing a new gun and belt.

"Steve," she cried, "leave this town with me at once."

"Don't worry, sis. I'm not crazy. I'm not looking for Curly. He'd eat me at one gulp — he's not in town."

Even as the boy spoke, she saw the colour drain from his face. She followed his eyes and saw Curly Watson step from the hotel and start toward Steve.

"So yuh got yuh a gun," Curly cried. "Get busy, then, and use it, 'cause I'm going to drop yuh."

The look in Curly's eyes appalled Madge. She looked wildly about for help. She saw Jimmy Ashton coming toward them slowly. She felt she could expect no help from him. The sheriff! Where was the sheriff? Several men stepped from a saloon and watched Curly and Steve. Madge made a desperate effort to call to them for help, but only a strangled cry came from her lips. She held out shaking hands toward Curly.

The breed's hand flashed on the way to his gun. He yanked it free, but even as he raised it, Madge saw a startled look come into his face. He staggered, and his gun exploded as it dropped from his hand. Curly turned and walked like a drunken man toward the hotel. He fell forward and sprawled on the steps.

For an instant Madge was too stunned to move. Then her eyes flashed toward Steve. She saw her brother still tugging to free his gun from its holster. Farther on she saw Jimmy Ashton with a smoking gun in his hand. At first she did not recognize him, for he seemed old, very old. His face was lined with countless wrinkles and his eyes were pools of yellow fire.

124

As Jimmy returned the smoking gun to the sheath beneath his arm, his face grew young again, and his eyes lost their fire. Madge gave a hysterical cry.

"Thank heaven, you killed the beast!"

She staggered toward Jimmy, clasped him in her arms, kissed him, and then fainted.

CHAPTER
FOURTEEN

The Call

That night Slim sat on the verandah, with his spurred heels cocked on the railing, and stared across the silver, moonlit plain to the far-distant hills. Suddenly turning to Old Doc, he growled :

"You have got to do something."

"About Madge?" Old Doc chuckled. "Now, Jimmy says women is like hosses —"

Slim interrupted.

"To hell with Jimmy. I tell you, after what happened to-day, she'll be falling in love with him."

"Son," Old Doc said seriously, "I'm right sorry for that little cuss. I wish she would fall in love with him, 'cause that would be a sign he's alive."

"Sorry — hell," Slim snorted. "I tell you, you're overplaying your hand. I never see such a look in a woman's eyes as she has when she looks at him."

"I've seen it," Old Doc sighed. "Women have it when they look at a grave. Son, women don't fall in love with dead men — they mourn for them, and that's what Madge is doing for Jimmy. She knows he is dead inside."

Slim Dent considered this for a moment. As he was about to ask for further explanations of Old Doc's statement, the old man whispered:

"Shut up — I'm goin' to be mighty mean and listen."

Slim heard the sound of two people entering the lighted room behind him. He glanced through the open window and saw Jimmy and Madge.

He heard Jimmy say: "Madge, read that."

Came a moment of silence, then Madge whispered:

"How horrible — but I suppose it was necessary."

"Reckon it was." Then Jimmy added without expression: "You know that you and Slim killed those men."

"I!" Madge exclaimed in surprised horror.

"Yes — you. You can't hide behind the hangman. It was your money that paid him. You can't say you bribed someone to do something that you wouldn't have done yourself, if necessary. You and the rest of the people told the hangman to put the noose around their necks."

"Yes," Madge said slowly — thoughtfully. "I see what you mean — we are all responsible." Then she added quickly: "But it was done lawfully."

"Lawfully — yes — but what is the law?"

"Why —"

"Listen — just because something is written in a book — that doesn't make it law. If someone wrote in the law book that everyone had to get drunk each day — that wouldn't make you get drunk."

"No."

"'Cause you wouldn't believe it was the law. Just because it is *not* written in a book that it means

127

hanging to get caught with a straight iron — that does not mean it is *not* the law, because it is the people what makes the law."

"Yes — I see that — now," Madge said slowly.

"And the law of this country says you can defend yourself and kill without bribing a hangman to do it for you. Now in New York the people say you can't — so that is the law there. Now when I dropped Curly to-day — the sheriff didn't do nothin', 'cause folks figgered I done right."

"Yes — it is the community's opinions that make the law," Madge spoke judicially. "I have been a little fool."

"Now, I'm askin' you, what are you goin' to do to get Red off the Double X Ranch?"

Madge thought for a moment.

"I will try the law — but I'm afraid it will do nothing."

"Remember, folks will back your play if you get a bunch of gunmen and kick Casey out."

"I can't do that. I can't ask men to pay with their blood for my stupidity."

"Good girl!" Jimmy was pleased. "Suppose I fixed things so yuh got back yuhr ranch and no one was hurt?"

"You couldn't do that."

"If I did," Jimmy insisted, "would yuh do something for me?"

"Yes."

"Even if it meant standin' before a parson?"

Slim waited breathlessly for her answer and, when a soft affirmative came, he went cold all over. Old Doc

128

reached out and grasped his arm. Talonlike fingers bit into it, as the old man whispered:

"Son, yuh misplay this hand and yuh lose that girl forever."

"Damn him — standing up with a parson — I'll kill him. The girl's in love with the little runt," Slim gritted.

"Yuh damn fool," Doc cried disgustedly. "He's just dealt yuh four aces, and yuh don't know how to play them."

Slim had been too busy conquering the green monster to give heed to Madge's troubles with Red. He now considered this and wondered what part he could play in the winning back of her ranch. This led him to realize that Madge's promise had been given on a condition, and he felt relieved when he realised that the condition was impossible.

To win back her ranch without bloodshed — that was impossible. Red Casey would never give up without a fight.

Old Doc waited until Madge had left Jimmy, then he entered the ranch house. He found the room, where the two had been, empty.

When Old Doc entered the bedroom back of his office, he found the boy sitting on the side of the bed, pulling off his moccasins.

"Yuh tell me what happened over to the Double X," he said.

"The gal was plumb scornful. She asks Red why for he has a ruction with Curly over to Twin Creek. Red says 'cause Curly was aimin' to steal some of the

129

Double X range." The boy grinned, then rolled a cigarette.

"And?" Old Doc demanded impatiently.

"Her majesty gets plumb haughty and tells Red he is fired. But Red gets positive in his talk — says he fought for that ranch and, if the gal didn't want it, he'd keep it hisself. And then he says, cool-like, he's got papers to prove the major left him four-fifths of it and he offers to buy the gal out. She goes gallopin' to town to see the sheriff. But th' sheriff explains that he can't do nothin', an' the girl commences to see that things is too strong for her. Then Curly jumps young Steve —"

"An' yuh drops Curly," Doc interrupted.

"Yeh," the boy said carelessly. "And instead of turnin' away from me, 'cause I was a murderer, she throws her arms around me and kisses me right before the whole town. She sure knows now she can't change the ways of a whole State, just 'cause she says so."

"Yuh figure Red's aimin' to stick to the Double X?" Old Doc demanded anxiously.

"Yep!" the boy said positively. "Red will sure stick, and I can't say I blames him."

"I ain't denyin' —" Doc admitted. "I ain't denyin' there's a certain reasonableness in Red's actions. He's sure human — wantin' to hang on to what he fought for. And he sure glories in battle and sudden death. If he decides to fight, it's sure goin' to be hard to get the Double X back for that fool girl."

"Reckon I can fix that," the boy said confidently.

130

"Hell — don't be a darned fool. Red's got the toughest bunch of killers that ever rid together. They're even too much for yuh, unless yuh gets them separate."

The boy's eager eyes became clouded, and the smile left his face. He was old again, suddenly.

"Can't blame folks if they thinks I takes delight in killin' — but I don't," he said sadly.

Old Doc hastened to square himself.

"Huh, Jim, I didn't mean nothin'. Now looka here — I —"

"Huh, forget it," the boy interrupted with a smile.

Old Doc thought for a moment, then said: "I knows that gal, and she won't take back her ranch if there's blood spilt getting it."

"I aim to run Red out without no killin'."

"Sure." Old Doc was sarcastic. "We sends him a billy-doo and asks him polite to drift off the range."

The boy grinned.

"That's what we'll do."

"How?"

"Yuh gets Red to consent to a public sale of the Double X. The sheriff auctions off Red's share and Madge's share. I'm aimin' to fix things so Red won't do no biddin', and Madge will buy back her four-fifths what Red stole, darn cheap."

Old Doc pondered for a moment, then shook his head.

"Nope, can't be did."

"Doc, yuh ever hear a pack of wolves howl?" the boy asked.

The older man nodded.

131

"Sort o' frightenin' if yuh is all alone?"

"Sure is."

Old Doc stared at the boy with growing curiosity.

"That's why Red won't draw cards at the auction."

With that the boy climbed into bed and, turning his face to the wall, promptly went to sleep.

"He's the most aggravatin' little cuss I ever see — he plumb arouses your curiosity until it's active like a woman's, then he goes to sleep," Old Doc complained to Slim Dent, after he had related the conversation to him.

"He's talkin' kid's stuff," Slim insisted. "We got to gather a bunch of Texas gunmen and shoot Red off that ranch."

"Can't be did without a killin'."

"What of it?"

Doc shook his head.

"That gal realizes she's a fool! Now what kind of gal would you think her, if she let a lot of men get killed, just because she had been a fool?"

"But what are you goin' to do?" Slim growled.

"Got to let Jim try his play."

"Him?" Slim was contemptuous.

Old Doc chuckled.

"Madge ain't the only fool hereabouts. But I'll admit I'm plumb curious how he's goin' to do it."

The more Old Doc puzzled over it, the more curious he grew. He could get no word out of Jimmy in spite of abject pleading.

Several days later, an accident gave the answer to the riddle. "Baldy" Small, about to carry the ranch's mail bag sixty miles to Bolton, opened it by request of "One Wing," who, in a thoughtless moment, had written a sentimentally binding proposal to a certain young lady and, on second thought, had decided to retrieve it. While Baldy was pawing the letters over in his search, he saw several of the names and addresses of which made him whistle and hasten to Old Doc.

"Who to hell is writin' to them fellows?" he blurted out.

Old Doc not only looked over the letters pointed out by Baldy, but every letter in the bag. He became thoughtful and then suddenly grinned.

"The little devil! So that's his game — the Wolf is sendin' out the pack call." He cautioned Baldy: "You be damned careful with those letters — they're important — you mail 'em careful — and keep your mouth shut."

CHAPTER
FIFTEEN

Lions and Lambs

On the day before the now famous auction of the Double X Ranch, the town of Bolton began to fill. Cots in the hotel were bringing "four bits" each. Curious crowds, filled with the exciting prospect of a fight, thronged the streets. Before night, men were offering a dollar for the privilege of sleeping on the floor. The hitching rail before the Lone Star, for the first time in its history, was filled with lean sweat-covered ponies, whose owners crowded the bar, quenching their thirst and awaiting the morrow to quench their curiosity.

All were wondering what Old Doc intended to do.

"Huh, I know him," a squat cattleman declared. "You can't tell me he's goin' to lay down and let Red Casey gather in those cows, 'thout makin' a play."

"If he did, the old major would sure haunt him," another vouched.

"That's true enough," cut in a third. "But Red's a fighter, and I reckon you couldn't gather any tougher bunch of punchers than his if you combed the whole of Texas."

"They sure are tough."

"Just look what they did to the Frying Pan bunch. I reckon Old Doc —" The squat cattleman became conscious that someone was crowding him, so he interrupted himself and cried sharply to the intruder, a tall man: "Who you crowdin'?"

"I'm right sorry, mister, but I'm tryin' to reach that drink," the man replied coolly contrarily.

The cattleman was about to continue with a few pointed remarks, when he noted the bartender. With apoplectic face and popping eyes, that worthy was shaking his head vigorously. The cattleman glanced again and more carefully at the tall man's back. Instantly he changed his attitude.

"Plenty of room! Plenty of room!" he said heartily.

Then he nudged his companions, who gulped their drinks and faded hastily to the back of the room. There they conversed in whispers.

They were joined by Tillman, the fat proprietor of the Comfort Hotel. Tillman whispered excitedly:

"Say, do you know who just rode in and asked for a room?" He paused impressively before he added: "Jesse Ryan and 'Dad' Evans!"

But the news which ordinarily would have caused his audience to bristle with excitement, strangely enough, seemed to affect them little.

"Huh," said one. "Who's them? Just run your eyes along that there box and stop 'em when you sight that big fellow with the curly hair and the little runt with the whiskers."

The proprietor stared at the two indicated. One was very tall, muscular and agile, with yellow hair and hard,

135

blue eyes. The other had the figure of an undersized boy. A bristly, aggressive beard almost hid his wide, loose mouth and pug nose. Tillman was awe-struck.

" 'Bad Bill' Rogers and Jack-twin Allen!" he whispered.

By this time most of those present had become aware of the presence of two of the most famous of all the frontier sheriffs. A hush settled over the room. It was followed by a stifled murmur, when two more men stepped through the door and stood with their backs against the wall, while their bright eyes searched the crowd.

One was a bright-faced, pleasant-looking boy with curly hair and prominent buck teeth. The other, a few years older, was of medium height and dark. Both fixed their eyes on Jack-twin Allen and allowed them to rest there.

"The 'Yuma Kid' and Pete Borden."

The whisper swept the room. All there knew that there was no love lost between the Allen twins and the Yuma Kid's gang, so all prepared to duck if trouble started.

A moment later, when the small, whiskered man swung about and walked toward them, the crowd surged aside, out of the line of fire. Then it gasped with sheer amazement. Instead of going for his gun, the Yuma Kid thrust out his hand and shook that of Allen.

"You here because Jim sent for you?" Jack-twin Allen asked with a smile.

"Yep — he saved me from the Apaches once, and I promised him I'd come a-runnin' if he ever called for help," the Kid said.

136

"I had a rope around my neck when he butts in, and so I'm here," grunted Pete Borden.

"An' old scores is forgot until to-morrow?" Jack Allen asked.

"That's the agreement." The Kid grinned. "After to-morrow, when yuh sees me, come a-shootin'."

Allen nodded and the three turned to the bar. Bad Bill shook hands with the newcomers, and the pop-eyed bartender served the four with a drink.

The squat cattleman shook his head in wonder and muttered:

"That girl, Miss Madge, said peace and good-will was coming to this country —"

"And the lions shall lay down with the lambs," some one remarked, as Jesse Ryan and Dad Evans swung into the room and, with widespread grins, joined the four at the bar. For they were not only sworn enemies of the Yuma Kid's gang, but of the Allen boys as well.

"I'm dry!" the squat cattleman exclaimed feebly. Followed by his friends, he staggered toward the bar.

"Double slugs, friends!" he ordered.

The bartender skilfully spun glasses and a bottle toward them, then, with a conscious effort to make his voice sound casual, he said:

"Mr. Tillman, shake hands with Frank Jones, Tom Cole, and Charlie Pitts. They was askin' about a room to sleep in — told 'em you would fix 'em up."

Tillman was about to blurt out that he was full up, thought better of it and, after gravely shaking hands with the notorious outlaws, stammered:

137

"Guess I can fix you up — you can have number two and three."

A little later he whispered to the squat cattleman and his friends: "Hope you don't mind me givin' them your rooms."

"What to hell does this all mean?" the bartender enquired. "There's Pat Rinehart!"

"Where?"

"That tall, skinny fellow; and he's sittin' with Ben Thomas, King Fisher, and Tomlinson, that Texas sheriff; and Bob and Frank Lewis are over there by the door. Them there are all strangers to this metropolis, and each of 'em carries a hell of a big reward. I reckon, if you could collect it all, you'd have a hundred thousand dollars."

"And you'd spend it in hell."

"The party would be plumb complete if you had that little hellion of a Wolf, Jim-twin Allen, here."

The squat cattleman nodded.

"Funny they should all turn up the same day."

Madge, Old Doc, and Slim arrived in town on the following morning, five minutes after Red Casey and his crew of hard-bitten cowpunchers had swung from their sweating ponies before the Comfort Hotel. He had wisely held his men out of town overnight. He had no desire to have a battle start prematurely. He and his men still stood about the street in little groups, when Madge and her party rode up. The girl passed him, head held high, scornful. Slim Dent's face was tense with suppressed wrath; his mouth was drawn into a thin line, and his eyes blazed as they met Red Casey's laughing, reckless, blue ones. With an effort he controlled himself, gave Red a curt nod, swung past him, and followed Madge into the hotel.

The town loafers, despairing of seeing a battle, sneered, but there were others who wondered. Slim's courage was well known. If he restrained himself, it was for a purpose. Curiosity was aroused. Some of the loungers glanced toward Old Doc in an effort to read the answer in his face. But what they saw there only puzzled them the more. His long, lean face was beaming; his eyes, from beneath the shaggy brows, twinkled with inward mirth, as he carelessly questioned Red Casey about the condition of the Double X stock.

"They're doin' fine," Red replied shortly.

"I'm glad to hear it."

Old Doc's sincerity was apparent to all, and it made Red thoughtful. His eyes sparkled. Maybe there was going to be trouble. But what could Old Doc do? He had no men to fight for him — the time for battle was past. Yet — Old Doc was joyously confident. Red was a man of action, and anything he could not understand disturbed him. He was still puzzling over the affair, when "Scarface," his foreman, interrupted his thoughts.

"There's somethin' queer goin' on — you better talk to the boys," he growled.

Red nodded and swung about, curtly ordering his men to follow. He walked across the wide, dusty street and vanished into the Red Star Saloon.

"Say, there goes Jack-twin Allen," someone cried.

All present stared with open curiosity and admiration, as the famous little gun fighter strutted into the street.

"Gosh! Look at those whiskers!"

Jimmy Ashton piped this sacrilege, and those near him growled a caution to his impudence, which Jimmy ignored.

"Ain't he dignified? Look at those heels, tryin' to make hisself into a man's size."

He turned with a broad grin to his audience, who moved uneasily and breathed freely only when it became apparent that Jack-twin Allen had not heard the insults.

"He's too damned dignified! I've got to ruffle his feathers," shouted Jimmy. The boy moved with a quickness that baffled clutching hands. With an ear-splitting whoop he was upon the little sheriff's back.

The crowd herded toward places of safety. Jack would annihilate that presumptuous kid. But over their shoulders they saw a spectacle that caused them to pause in wonder. The two small figures were rolling like playful puppies in the deep dust. At last Jack managed to pin his opponent on his back and proceeded to wash the impudent face with thick mud.

"Yes, sir," Scarface said, as he related the incident later that night. "Those two used fightin' language for ten minutes and never repeated themselves once. It was the finest exhibition of fancy swearin' I ever see. Folks was wantin' to duck till they see that those fightin'

140

words were just terms of endearment. Those two sure care a heap for each other."

The two dust-covered little men scrambled to their feet. Their faces were alight with broad grins, as they pushed through the laughing crowd to the hitching racks, where two mean, scrawny, grey horses were tied up at one post.

"The old mare looks meaner than ever," Jack cried.

"That old bag of bones is the meanest horse west of the Mississippi," Jimmy cried proudly.

"Ain't you forgetting her brother?" Jack-twin Allen's eyes were shining as they rested on Jimmy. "Does he eat pie, too?"

"You wait."

Jimmy vanished into the hotel to reappear shortly with a large pie. The horses snapped back at him and at each other, as he, to the amused wonderment of the crowd of spectators, fed them the pie.

"That's a new one on me," Bad Bill said. "First time I ever see horses eat pie."

"Horses!" Jimmy cried dolefully. "Those ain't horses — they're billy goats. Look at this shirt — they plumb eat it up."

He poked discontentedly at the holes in his shirt, then followed Jack into the hotel.

"If Jack shaved his whiskers, he'd look just like that kid," a cow-puncher confided to "Tall Ed".

Tall Ed grinned.

"Maybe — maybe you couldn't tell 'em apart."

Madge, from the shelter of the hotel parlour, had watched the spectacle of the feeding of the horses with amusement. She, of all those present, saw beneath the surface of things and knew that it was the love of a lonely man for his only companions.

"Poor Jimmy," she sighed.

Later, when Red Casey reappeared and started for the scene of action, he noticed the laughing crowd and inquired what had happened.

"Some one jumped Jack-twin Allen," Scarface explained. "There was no gunnin'. They was old friends by the way they swore at each other."

If Red had witnessed the scene, or if Scarface had thought it sufficiently important to mention that the bandaged kid who was staying up at Old Doc's was the one who had jumped Jack-twin Allen, it is certain that Casey would have guessed the truth. Even if he had, it is doubtful if he could have done anything that would have materially changed the result. As it was, he walked toward the schoolhouse, quite unaware that he was to be offered an opportunity of a fight that even his stout heart would decline. For there is no pleasure to be gained from certain annihilation.

If Red was confident, there were others who suspected the truth, and they sternly forbade their womenfolk to attend the auction.

CHAPTER
SIXTEEN

Until Next Time

The schoolhouse had been carefully built to serve as a theatre if necessary. The body of the building was crowded with chairs, and, in order to furnish further seating capacity, long boards had been placed on boxes and barrels. Every seat was occupied, and the doorway and walls were crowded by the late-comers. The room was filled to suffocation, yet strangely enough, there was an empty space adjacent to Casey and his hard-faced, heavily armed cow-punchers. These sat in lonely state at the right end, close to the raised platform. Old Doc and Jimmy were seated to the left.

Curiosity was rampant, for those present couldn't believe that Old Doc would allow his neice to be robbed in such a barefaced manner — yet all shook their heads. How could he stop the sale at this late date? It was impossible for him to outbid Red Casey, for the latter could run the price as high as he wished, since he would be buying his own property.

"Gents!" The sheriff banged on the table, then, rising from his place on the platform, he became confused at the battery of faces that confronted him. He stuttered, then roared.

"You all savvy why we are here. Let's get started."

Abruptly he threw himself into his chair and for the want of something better to do, banged with his makeshift gavel — the butt end of a six-shooter — on the table.

Slim Dent, from his position at the rear of the oblong room, where he sat to the left of Madge — Tall Ed was on her right — noticed the sheriff's blundering embarrassment and, in spite of himself, he smiled rather sulkily. He shifted his gaze from the sheriff to Old Doc, who, even though seated, towered above the diminutive Jimmy. He had no idea what their plans were. He squirmed internally at the role for which he had been cast. Old Doc promised that there would be no gun play, but just the same Slim felt slighted. He had been refused a place on the fighting line. He squirmed the more when he was obliged to admit the justice of Old Doc's statement.

"Sorry, son — but I can't trust you. If you or some other fool made the wrong play, a number of men would die. Ordinarily I would want you close to me — but in this play you're too damned mad at Red and might go off half-cocked, so you got to stand aside and let Jimmy play the hand."

That was the rub — Jimmy was playing the hand — that little, cocksure bantam rooster. Abruptly Slim snapped out of his reverie.

"No more bids, gents?" The sheriff paused, and his eyes strayed to Old Doc, then he continued: "Miss Madge's one-fifth share of the Double X Ranch is sold to Mr. Casey for four thousand five hundred dollars."

A strange whistling noise, as men exhaled their long-held breaths, filled the room. A battery of eyes sought the back of Old Doc's grey head. When he made no sign, each man turned and looked questioningly at his neighbour.

Red Casey cursed. The lack of opposition made what he had done appear contemptible. He had expected a fight — a fight that would have satisfied even his rambunctious soul. In fact, he had schemed to secure control of the Double X for the love of a fight quite as much as for any desire to get the ranch. He was both disgusted and disappointed.

After he had recovered from his first shock of surprise, Slim flashed a look at Madge and was puzzled at the serene confidence he saw in her face. Tall Ed grinned.

"Hold your horses, Slim — the thing ain't over yet," he whispered.

"What can he do now? He's waited too long," Slim growled.

Madge turned and looked at him questioningly, searchingly.

"I'm afraid I'm going to have to keep that promise," she said.

Slim's eyes flashed. His face grew taut; he felt Madge's cool, slender hand in his. He clutched it savagely and then was immediately bewildered, for she made no effort to withdraw it. His heart leaped in his throat, when her eyes met his. They were inscrutable. Damn women, anyway! What did she mean? He hung

145

on to her hand like a drowning man to the proverbial straw.

"Now, ladies and gents," the sheriff began, "Mr. Casey's four-fifths share of the Double X is up for sale. What am I bid?"

"Four thousand five hundred dollars."

Old Doc drawled his bid and his voice was low, yet it had the effect of a cannon shot in that crowded room. A ripple of whispered exclamations swept across the audience. All fixed their expectant eyes first on Old Doc and then on Red Casey. Surprise for a moment swept the latter off his feet, and before he could recover, Jimmy was up beside the sheriff. His eyes were laughing, and a broad grin was on his face. It was the first time that most of those present had seen the little man without his bandages. As Red stared, memory knocked at the door of his mind, ominously. He had seen that face before.

Again a ripple of excitement swept across the room as eyes switched from the freckled face to a bill tacked to the right wall. But it was not the heading of the bill, which offered a five-thousand-dollar reward, "dead of alive," that attracted their eyes. It was the photograph below the description. Men arose and sought less conspicuous positions in the rear of the hall.

Jimmy's voice shrilled through the big room.

"Mr. Sheriff, ladies and gents, before this biddin' goes any further I would like to spout a few words. Perhaps you'll think, as the lawyers say, that they're not relevant — but I'm goin' to spout just the same. Now I asks you all to think back to the time when Major

Steward first came into this country. There was bad Indians — and white men that was worse. There wasn't no law and less justice. The way to the sheriff was long and to Mr. Colt plumb short. Folks were impatient — so Mr. Colt talked a lot more than the law.

"The major had to fight, and — lucky for him — he had a foreman that could also fight. Both the major and Red fought and fought. Then one day the major ran into a slug, and Miss Madge came out to take command. She looks around and says: 'These folks is just crazy — they think they're still living in the wilderness and they think it's necessary to pack guns.' Miss Madge looks around and sees that the cowboy is blind like a hombre that stays out in the desert too long. Yes, the folks hereabouts is blind — 'cause they can't see that the old times is gone; that law and justice, peace and goodwill has come in. Miss Madge, she tells them, but they sniff and don't believe her any more than if she was a howling yearling."

Jimmy paused for breath and grinned at Red Casey. Red was beginning to realize that perhaps there was to be a fight after all. As he waited for the other to play his cards, his eyes twinkled with an unholy light.

Slim's face was blank, he resented Jimmy's allusion to Madge's mistaken philosophy of law and justice. A ripple of amusement had swept across the audience at the boy's insistence that the old times had gone. One man guffawed loudly.

"Yes, ladies and gents," Jimmy continued, "while folks hereabouts refused to believe in Miss Madge's law and justice — word got out about the country — and

147

men, who is plumb tired of toting guns, says: 'I'll go ask that gal for a job and try that business of peace and goodwill.' Some of them came a long ways. So if you folks don't mind, I'd like to introduce you all to these peace-loving hombres and ask you what to do about it.

"I'd better start with the most respectable one of these gents. So I'll present the old marshal of Dodge City to Miss Madge, first:

"Mr. Bad Bill Rogers."

Bad Bill, tall and powerful, arose, bowed with absolute composure, then took a position a little to the left of Jimmy. People stared and then switched their eyes to the next man called by Jimmy.

"You folks has heard of the Wyoming sheriff, Jack-twin Allen. He's the gent who's so ashamed of his face that he covers the same with a scrubbing brush. And don't none of you ever tell him you know he's growed five inches on the heels of his boots, 'cause he's plumb sensitive."

"Ha, ha," someone laughed raucously. Then, when the unknown became abruptly silent at a glance from Jack-twin Allen, the whole house arose and shouted their mirth till the ceiling shook.

"You damn little fool! I washed your face this morning and, when I get you outside, I'll give you a whole mud bath," the sheriff growled at Jimmy.

"I reckon yuh has all heard about Pat Rinehart, so it ain't necessary for me to spout about him."

Pat Rinehart unfolded himself like a ruler and took his place to the right of Jack-twin Allen. The crowd snickered, for the border sheriff was unusually tall, six

148

feet six inches, and he and the huge Bad Bill sharply accentuated the size of Jack-twin Allen. The diminutive Wyoming sheriff flushed, then grinned, as he glanced at his two brother officers who towered above him.

"Mr. Tomlinson, the sheriff what makes Texas behave," Jimmy introduced, as a slender, hard-eyed man took his place beside Pat Rinehart.

"I'm askin' Miss Madge's pardon, 'cause the rest of her cow-punchers ain't what folks calls respectable. Frank Jones, I'm sorry to say, is a sort of uncle of mine. Tom Cole, who folks call the human lead mine, is another, an' the Lewis boys is cousins — they ain't got no manners 'cause they has brought their rifles to this peace meetin'."

The Lewis brothers seldom used a short gun; they relied on their rifles, which they could use, even at close range, far more effectively and rapidly than most men can their six-shooters.

The audience had lapsed into silent awe, as one famous outlaw after the other arose from his place in the crowd and sauntered forward at the call of his name, to stand close to the boy on the platform.

"Yuh has all heard of the Yuma Kid and his side kick, Mr. Pete Borden," Jimmy continued. "Then there is Charlie Lewis, Jesse Ryan, Dad Evans, 'Doc' Tomlinson, and Mr. King Fisher hisself. These gents is all lookin' for good jobs where there is peace and goodwill, so's they won't have to pack their guns no more."

Name after notorious name rolled from Jimmy's glib tongue, until at last twenty famous outlaws and frontier

149

sheriffs stood in a row beside him. They faced Red Casey's band of open-mouthed riders.

A veritable gallery they made of fame and infamy. All were lone wolves — outlawed from the human pack. Men of blood, who lived by the gun and were doomed to die by the gun.

Tall Ed's eyes snapped with excitement. He whispered to Slim:

"Gosh, what do you think of that? Do you think Red Casey's goin' to call that hand?"

Slim shook his head.

"No, he's got *too much* nerve."

Jimmy's voice drawled on.

"Now, ladies and gents, what do you think? These here are peaceful men and have travelled far to work on this peace-and-good-will ranch. And they get here to find that Miss Madge has no ranch to work on. So I suggest" — his words here were crisply cut in emphasis and directed at Red Casey's corner — "seein' that law and justice has arrived, Mr. Sheriff knocks down that four-fifths of the Double X to Miss Madge for four thousand five hundred dollars."

As Jimmy ceased speaking, he moved quickly to a position in front of his dark-visaged, peace-loving friends. All those present, including Red Casey, observed that the ominous phalanx represented twice as many guns as men.

Thus far, buffoonery had been the keynote, but one false play by Red or any of his men would turn the place into a shambles. The front benches were vacated swiftly; people slipped out through the doors and windows. Those two groups of men were left facing each other in a room, empty, save for a few stragglers near the rear wall, whose curiosity had overcome fear, and by the little trio of Madge, Old Doc and Slim. There was a tense silence.

The joyful light of battle faded from Red's eyes, as he stared at the group of the most famous gunmen in the country. Bad Bill, the Allens, the Lewis boys, and the Yuma Kid were waiting his move with a sort of smiling indifference. He knew that one play on his part would send them into action with a speed that no eye could follow. He also noticed that King Fisher, Tomlinson, and the other men from Texas were straining at their leashes like terriers. Their eyes were filled with blood lust. They were the more dangerous, for they hoped that he would make a play, that he would do something that they could use as an excuse to begin the slaughter — and it would be slaughter. He was very close to death. His men were paralyzed from surprise. There were just two things he could do. He had but a second to decide, or one of his men might sneeze, and then the killers would accept it as an excuse to go for their guns.

The drawling voice of the sheriff cut into his consciousness.

"Any more bids?"

Red grimaced sourly and made a motion, as if throwing something away.

"Gents," he said, "my hand is in the discard."

"Reckoned you would," said Jimmy, grinning. Then, although he knew Red understood his meaning, for fear

151

that perhaps others might not, he added: "I knew you had nerve."

A less brave man, a man less sure of his own bravery, might have felt that it was necessary for him to prove that he had nerve. It takes something more than just physical nerve to back down, to admit you are beaten, in public.

Red swung toward Jack-twin Allen and laughed.

"You promised to give him a mud bath — make it two — one for me."

There was a general guffaw. The two sides mixed. The crowd swarmed back into the room, in excited good humour.

Slim Dent had watched the proceedings with mixed feelings. He had felt surprise, as the notorious gunmen gathered — growing understanding of their meaning and of Jimmy's plan. Jimmy now made his way through the crowd to the side of Slim and Madge.

"You made me a promise, Miss Madge," he whispered. "You ready to keep it?"

She hesitated for the fraction of a second. "Yes," she said softly.

"Come on, then. The parson's waiting," commanded Jimmy.

Slim's face paled with fury. So this was what it had meant — that promise. Jimmy had saved the ranch because he wanted to marry Madge. She was the stake. The little snake had called these gunmen to his aid to win. Slim took one step forward, met Madge's look of scorn, and paused with clenched hands, irresolute.

"You mean you wish me to marry the jealous gentleman who is glowering at you," the girl smiled.

Jimmy grinned. Slim dropped his hands, sheepishly. He had been a fool. He found a sudden liking for that loose, broad grin.

"I always knew you meant that," Madge said, and she added in a shy whisper: "I always intended to, anyway."

Slim gulped. Old Doc chuckled, and Jimmy nodded.

Five minutes later, Slim was legally married, though to speak truthfully, he was hardly present at his own wedding. He was in a distant fog, presided over by a loosely grinning, good-natured face. Madge admitted later that perhaps she was really married to Jimmy, for it was he who efficiently prompted all necessary responses during the ceremony.

The celebration, after the marriage, lasted until dawn. But hardly had the night flung its blanket of purple over the peaks, when Madge's new cow-punchers silently deserted their jobs and slipped away.

None had seen how and whence they came; none saw them leave.

They were wolves and they travelled alone, along secret paths.

They had answered the call of the pack, and now, once more, they dispersed to take up their lonely lives.

By accident Madge, Old Doc and Slim overheard the farewell of the twin brothers.

"Where you headin' for, Jack?"

"Wyoming. And you?"

"I'm hittin' for the Painted Desert."

"So long."

"Until next time."

The listeners knew as well as the brothers that, by all the laws of fate and chance, there would be no next time for those two.

There was silence for a moment, then Jack, spurs jingling, noisily clumped from the room.

As Madge entered, Jimmy swung about, and her heart went out in sympathy at the haggard lines of his face. Jimmy, to-night, was a hopeless, weary old man. He had aged many years since that morning.

"Ma'am," he said tonelessly, "I'm right sorry that I fooled you, but it was sort of nice here — those bandages — I felt like a different man. I'm not askin' you to forgive me for foolin' you, because you're right about the way you feel about folks like me."

"I have nothing to forgive," Madge interrupted, as she laid her hand on his.

He stared at her in bewilderment. He said simply: "I'm Jim-twin Allen."

"The White Wolf." Her eyes were shining. "I've known that all the time."

She reached out her hand and impulsively stroked his hair.

"You poor, lonely boy," she said softly. "You made me happy, you have managed my affairs, you have married me off. Isn't there anything I can do to help you — marry Snippets?"

He held out his hands to her.

"Ma'am, my hands is stained. Men like me can't marry. I'm of the wolf breed."

154

"I or any other woman would be proud to take them in hers," she cried passionately and seized his hands in hers. After a time she added: "Where are you going from here?"

"I don't know."

"Jim, you haven't given up?" she demanded.

"A gent gets tired of drawin' two spots all the time."

"Oh, the pity of it," she thought to herself, "that a man who wanders through life bringing happiness to others should have so little for himself."

Old Doc and Slim swung from their position in the doorway and tiptoed away, silently. It is not good for men to see another man cry. Jimmy was crying. They walked to the farthest corral and climbed to the topmost rail; they hooked their high heels about a post and stared at the far-off mountains.

"Jealous?" Old Doc inquired gruffly.

Slim laughed.

"Not any — and if I was, I reckon it would do me no good — the Grey Killer."

Old Doc shook his head.

"I told you, son, he'd wash you lily-white by comparison."

Slim nodded gloomily.

"Women are hell!"

Again Old Doc shook his head.

"No — they're like hosses!"

CHAPTER
SEVENTEEN

An Attack

The squat adobe house stood like an inverted box in the centre of the arid valley. Leaden hail beat against its walls, ringed its narrow windows, and sent up spurts of dust around it. From the circle of rocks about the house came puffs of smoke, while the echo of rifle fire drummed against the slopes of the valley.

Farther back, on the crests of the hills, groups of mounted men looked on at the fight and watched for a cloud of dust that would warn of an approaching force to relieve the besieged.

The house itself appeared to be deserted. There came no answering fire from its windows. Little by little, the gun fire from the surrounding ring died away, and silence reigned over the valley. The men who were attacking had grown tired of aimless shooting. They crouched behind sheltering rocks and watched the windows for a target.

One of the mounted men on the crest of the hill shook his clenched fists and broke into furious profanity. He was a short, fat man. His high-crowned sombrero was heavy with silver and gold ornaments; his costume was gaudy, and his belt bristled with weapons.

The men about him shrank away. In one of his insane rages the "Tiger of the Border" was as likely to strike a friend as a foe.

"*Madre de Dios!* What do those fools down there? Do they think this is the time of the siesta?"

"Doubtless, those in the house are all dead," suggested one of his lieutenants, trembling.

The Tiger drew one of his pearl-handled guns and glared at the speaker. The young Mexican paled and glanced appealingly at the other bandit officers, but he saw no help in their faces.

"*Madre de Dios!* Help me!" he murmured to himself.

The fat Mexican outlaw chieftain mastered his rage with an effort and returned the gun to his belt.

"For three hours we have been here. You call yourselves soldiers of liberty. You are swine, all of you! There are but three men in that house. There are two hundred of you, and you tell me that you think perhaps the three gringos are dead. *Sangre de Cristo!* Take men! Beat down the door if they are dead. Show me their bodies. If they live, kill them. Go! Go at once. But remember, if a hair of my wife's head is hurt, I will cut your heart out."

"Yes, general, but if we —"

The young lieutenant stammered, then grew silent. He had no desire to lead a charge against that house. The sprawled figures in the cleared space about it bore silent testimony to the marksmanship of the three men within.

157

He thought rapidly, then added: "But, general, in a direct attack the 'Golden Rose,' your wife, might be struck by a chance bullet."

"For three hours we have been here. Do you forget we are north of the Rio Grande? At any moment Yankee soldiers may come. Have you remembered that?" The Tiger's voice was heavy with sarcasm.

The young lieutenant knew that well, but he did not care how soon the American soldiers came. There was no loot to be had in the capture of that house, only the general's wife. It would be better to let the gringos keep the Golden Rose, as the girl was called, than to face certain death in an attempt to batter down the doors.

"Come, have you a plan?" snarled the general, "or are you talking to gain time? Are you afraid to attack because the Wolf is in there?"

"The Wolf never misses," the lieutenant said to himself.

The Tiger of the Border guessed his thoughts, and his lips drew back in a snarl.

"So you fear the Wolf?"

"General! No, general," the lieutenant screamed. "I only thought that we might parley."

"To what end?"

"We might send a flag and say if they will return the Rose we will let the others go."

"True, general," another bandit added quickly. "There's no loot to be gained. Only death for many, for the Wolf's fangs are deadly."

The general glared about at his men. He saw at once that all there sympathized with the lieutenant. Unless he wished to face a possibly mutiny, it would be necessary to remind them of, and share with them, a certain sum of money which he had hoped to keep for himself. He gazed about contemptuously.

"You jackasses! Have I not told you that the Wolf is there?" he demanded.

"That is true. There is no need to parley, then, for the Wolf would never surrender the girl!" another Mexican cried.

"He is a spawn of the devil and has no fear," still another added, and there was grudging admiration in his voice.

The Tiger of the Border was not pleased with this tribute to another man's courage. He glowered at his men. A boast of his own fearlessness lay on the tip of his tongue; but if he boasted, someone might suggest that he lead the attack on the house. He decided to change the subject.

"Idiots, but what you say is true. But it is not that of which I speak. This imbecile" — he glowered at the quaking lieutenant — "this imbecile said there was no loot to be gained. Have you forgotten there is a reward of twelve thousand dollars for Jim Allen, dead or alive?"

The men clustered about him, breaking into grins and cheers — all save the lieutenant who had been elected to lead the assault.

"Go, lieutenant, and fail not. If you fear the Wolf, remember the Tiger."

The young lieutenant turned his horse and trotted slowly down the hill. He dismounted some three hundred yards from the house and crawled among the rocks toward the circling line of riflemen. Quietly he gave his orders.

A few minutes later the hidden riflemen suddenly came to life. From the mouths of Mausers and Winchesters a hail of bullets spattered against the adobe walls.

At the first burst of that terrific fusillade, the three men within the adobe house sprang to the loopholes and peered out. All three had received slight wounds.

"Black" Saunders, a big, heavy man of forty, had been creased along the side of his head. A bloody bandage covered one of his deep-set, heavy-browed eyes. "Slats" Higgins, a slender man of twenty-five, had been hit in the left arm and wore it strapped to his side.

Jim-twin Allen, the third man, had been struck in the thigh by a ricochetting steel-nosed Winchester .303.

Beside the three men, there were two girls. Nina Tower was a petite blonde. The other girl, Alice, the wife of Black Saunders, was a little taller, but very slender.

The house consisted of three rooms. One large centre room had a door, two loopholes that faced the south and two windows facing north. At either end, doors led from it into the two smaller rooms. One of these had been used as a kitchen and the other as a living room. Both had outside doors and windows. All the windows in each room were boarded up, but the boards had been splintered and torn by bullets.

Each man had been assigned a room to defend. By common consent, Jim Allen took the large centre room.

This was not only the most important key in the defence, but also, because of its two windows and two loopholes, the most dangerous position.

At the first burst of firing, Allen, limping from one window to the other, peered carefully through them. The wound in his thigh was deep, but not dangerous. He went into the kitchen and looked at the three people there.

The two girls were huddled in one corner, while Slats Higgins squinted through one of the loopholes. Slats' face was grim as, in answer to a signal from Allen, he followed him into the centre room. Allen called to Black Saunders, who joined them from the living room.

"Reckon the greasers is gettin' ready to rush us," Allen said with a grin.

Black Saunders glowered at him.

"For the love of Pete, stop that fool grinnin'!" he growled.

"Shut up, Black," snapped Slats Higgins. "You might as well grin as fill the place full of gloom."

"Maybe so, but I figure we're all due to cash in and I, for one, don't see no sense in tryin' to fool ourselves about it. I'll fight as long as I can pull a trigger, but I ain't sayin' I long for no death fight."

"Shucks, we can stand them greasers off," Allen said confidently.

"Sure we can until night. Then it's good-bye for us," Black insisted gloomily.

"But before night we'll be —" Slats glanced at Allen and brought his remarks to an abrupt halt.

"We'll be what?" Black asked.

"Nothin'," Slats replied vaguely.

Allen glanced curiously at Slats. He had the impression that Slats' interrupted remarks concerned himself. Slats had almost revealed something he did not want Allen to know. The latter frowned and tried to puzzle out the answer.

He had met these two men and the two girls that morning, heading straight toward Death Mesa, a waterless waste that stretched for miles toward the north. Their horses were played out. It would have meant a horrible death for all four to have attempted to cross the mesa. When they told Allen that they were pursued by a large band of Mexican outlaws, he had attempted to guide them to safety. But their horses were too spent. One after the other they had fallen. Allen's greys alone had survived. He had given them to the two girls.

The Mexicans had overtaken them easily and they had been forced to take refuge in this empty adobe house.

Allen disliked Black Saunders from the first. He placed him as a bully and a brute. But Slats Higgins was different. Allen was unable to catalogue him. Slats had a likeable face and a ready smile, but he had a curious way of veiling his eyes at times, as though he feared they would reveal his thoughts.

Again Allen looked at him. This time, when Slats' eyes met his, they were frank and friendly. Allen's distrust died, and he grinned in return, putting aside his suspicions for the moment. There were other things to consider. It would be time enough to figure-out Slats when they had beaten off the Mexicans.

Besides, there were the two girls. Allen did not care much for Nina Tower's babyish ways. She should have been more frightened at the idea of being re-captured by the Tiger of the Border. Curiously enough, the idea did not seem to disturb Nina at all.

Alice Saunders' dark eyes were pools of terror, and she had begged her husband to kill her rather than let her fall into the hands of the Mexicans. Allen's eyes hardened, as he remembered Black's coarse answer to that request. Later, if they defeated the Mexicans he would talk to that brute.

"I was just wantin' to suggest to you gents that, when the greasers rush us, we pick off the ones what is the best dressed; 'cause, you see, the best fighters get the most loot, an' if you knock them off, the rest will run like rabbits. Just take your time and line your sights on every greaser who is gaudy."

Black Saunders snorted.

"Huh! You talk like we was babies."

Slats Higgins flashed a glance at Black and shook his head. Then he said smoothly:

"Black, we two are babies, compared to the Wolf, when it comes to a fight."

Slats' glance was not lost on Allen, but Allen could not quite interpret it. He knew that Slats' friendliness rang false. He glanced from one to the other. Then the rifle fire of the Mexicans increased in fury, and he dismissed the puzzle.

163

"I reckon that means they're getting ready to attack," he said.

The other two nodded and hurried to their posts. Allen limped to a loophole and glanced out.

He heard the shrill blast of a whistle, and suddenly the firing ceased. Then several high-hatted Mexicans sprang from their cover and headed for the house on a run. Others followed them. Allen grinned to himself. These last seemed none too eager to attack. He heard the bark of Winchesters from the rooms on either side of him and knew that Black Saunders and Slats Higgins were in action.

But he withheld his fire. He waited until the leading group of Mexicans was within sixty yards of the adobe hut; then his Winchester slid to his shoulder, and he fired so rapidly that a continuous stream of fire came from the barrel. He fired until a click told him the magazine was empty. As he stuffed fresh shells in he squinted through the smoke. What he saw satisfied him. The attack from the south side was over. The whole crowd, save those who sprawled and squirmed on the ground, were racing back to shelter.

Allen trotted to one of the windows, and thrust his rifle through the loophole. The Mexicans on this side were close — far too close. The leaders were scarcely fifteen yards from the adobe. A slender young Mexican, whom Allen recognized as an officer, led them.

CHAPTER
EIGHTEEN

Treachery

The Winchester sprang to Allen's shoulder. For a second he held the sights full on the lieutenant's chest. Then his finger squeezed the trigger. The Mexican's headlong run stopped as though he had collided with a wall. He turned, took two or three staggering steps, then fell face down in the dust. Allen waited for a second to see if the death of their officer would halt the rush of the Mexicans; but they came on. His rifle poured out another continuous stream of fire, bullets, and death.

Then the Mexicans' fierce cries ceased abruptly. With one accord, they swung about and ran frantically for shelter. Black appeared in the doorway and gave Allen a tigerish grin.

"We sure gave 'em plenty," he gloated. "I dropped two, and they never gave a wiggle after they was hit. Then I got another who was wounded when he was wriggling back to his friends."

Allen shrugged indifferently and began to clean his rifle.

Black peered through the window on the north side, then crossed to the south and looked out of one of the loopholes.

"You got five on one side and six on the other," he said with a mixture of awe and stupefaction.

"Yeah, one was an officer, judging by his dress," Allen said carelessly, as he pulled the oiled cloth through the barrel of his rifle.

Black's mouth dropped open; he stared at Allen. From all appearances, Allen thought nothing of taking eleven lives. Black realized that the indifference was not assumed. Allen's attitude seemed inhuman; it was as if he had the instincts as well as the eyes and ears of a predatory animal.

Black had lived all his life along the border. He had seen many men killed and had known many killers. He had three notches on his own gun. But when he killed, or when the killers he knew killed, they always displayed some sign of human emotion — joy, hatred, revenge, or regret. Never before had he seen anyone who killed like a wolf — thoughtlessly, remorselessly.

Allen guessed the other's thoughts. He looked up and shrugged.

"No, I ain't neither glad nor sorry I downed them gents. It had to be, 'cause of them gals. There ain't nothin' else to it," he said tonelessly.

Black Saunders shivered in spite of himself. He gave thanks that he was fighting with and not against the Wolf. He shook his head and went into the kitchen. His wife was huddled in one corner, watching Slats Higgins and Nina Tower. The two were whispering, and Alice was leaning forward, as though trying to catch their words. Black scowled at her and crossed to Slats and

Nina, who turned to face him. The girl laid a warning finger on her lips.

"What's he doing?" Nina pointed toward the centre room.

"The Wolf? He's cleaning his gun."

Black whispered the reply and questioned the others with his eyes.

"It's this way, Black. It's Nina's idea. You know that little runt's worth twelve thousand big cart wheels," Slats said, and his voice quivered with excitement.

Black nodded.

"Nina here has a plan to cash in on him," Slats continued.

Comprehension broke on Black Saunders. He shook his head. He was still under the spell cast by Allen.

"Not any. I ain't aimin' to tangle with no coffin," he said throatily.

"Coffin! You scared of him?" Nina demanded scornfully.

"I'm scared of the devil. I tell you he cashes a gent like me as you would a fly," Black said positively.

"You fool! Didn't I tell you Nina had a plan?" Slats asked impatiently.

"Nina can have a million plans, and I don't join in. That's flat. Besides, where'd we be without him? Do you realize he guarded two sides of this here adobe and downed eleven greasers?"

"We — I —" Slats grew silent, as he considered this part of the affair.

Even if they succeeded in taking Allen, it would mean their ruin. He looked hopelessly at Nina Tower.

Her small mouth curled disdainfully.

"I know the Tiger," she said. "He won't attack again, and, even if he does, his men are discouraged. You two could beat them off. What happens if you wait? The posse may come along any minute. Then, good-bye reward."

"The posse? You expect them?" demanded Black.

Slats nodded.

"Yeah, when I left Weston, I told Sam Stevens, my deputy, if I warn't back afore night to get a posse out and hunt for my trail. I started to tell you about it in there, but I figured I better not let Allen know about it."

Black frowned.

"I tell you, you can't get near him. You ever notice how he sort o' keeps slidin' just out of arm's reach? An' he's so darned fast with them guns, he'd sure down you afore you could get him."

"I know," Slats admitted.

Nina Tower ran lightly to the door of the big centre room and glanced within. A second later she came back.

"He must be in the other room looking out the window there."

Suddenly the babyish expression left her face. It grew hard; her eyes were like marbles, as she fixed them on Slats. Her voice was shrill and scornful.

"Look here, Mr. Slats Higgins, we aimed to get enough out of the Tiger to get married on, so I pretended to let him capture me and, to make it good, I took Alice, that cry-baby over there, with me."

168

Slats Higgins snarled an interruption.

"I never told you to marry the dirty greaser."

"It was a question of saying yes or having my throat cut."

"Maybe it was, and maybe it wasn't. Maybe you thought you could get more out of him by marrying him," Slats growled suspiciously.

"Look here!" the girl cried. "I ain't the kind to thrive on love and kisses. I'm telling you plain you can cash in on the Wolf or open that door and I'll go back to the Tiger."

"Well, I ain't takin' a hand!" Black cried. "You can go! I tell you, to monkey with the Wolf is all the same as makin' a playmate of a grizzly. I tell you, you can't get near him. He ain't human."

Nina snapped her fingers.

"Men are all the same. Maybe you can't get near enough to grab him, but I bet I can. I'd start crying and make believe I'm afraid, then tumble in his arms. He'll grab me and give me a chance to flip his guns out of the holsters. Then you can handle him with one hand."

Slats grinned in open admiration of this scheme. But Black was not so sure. Greed struggled with his fear for a moment; then he surrendered.

"All right, I'll draw cards," he said.

He looked at the girl and added vindictively: "I know the Wolf, and don't you think your yaller curls and baby-blue eyes will save you if this thing flops. You cash, too, and don't be foolin' yourself you don't."

For a moment the blood drained from Nina's cheeks; then she shrugged her shoulders.

"You three are planning to betray the White Wolf after he saved you?" Alice Saunders murmured.

They glared at her. All three had been so interested in their own discussion that they had forgotten her. In a panic they glanced from her to the door. They heard Allen singing to himself in the farther room.

"You open your trap and I'll —" Black left his threat unsaid, but his expression was eloquent.

His wife shrank away, but she held out her hand in appeal.

"You can't do this thing. He saved us — guided us here."

The men winced, but Nina Tower was of sterner stuff.

"He didn't save us," she snapped. "He told us not to try to cross Death Mesa. Then the Tiger came, and he had to stick with us to save himself."

"How can you talk like that? If it had not been for him we would all have died in the desert. Again and again he could have saved himself, but he always came back to help us. Our horses were played out. He could have gone on. His greys were still fresh. But he stayed with us. Black, you and Slats would have been killed in the last attack if it hadn't been for him." Alice turned in desperate appeal to her husband. "Tell me you won't do it."

"Do you think we're going to toss away twelve thousand dollars just for you?" cried Nina.

"Then I'll warn Allen," Alice said.

She started toward the door, but Black caught her by the shoulder, swung her about and struck her brutally.

170

She slumped to the floor and lay with her head against the wall. The two men stared down at her, then glanced up at Nina in time to see her hard expression change to one of softness as she gazed toward the door.

Slats was clutched by icy fear as he glanced over his shoulder and saw Allen standing in the doorway. To hide his panic, he stooped and gazed through the loophole. Black gaped at Allen.

Nina came to the rescue. She stooped and cuddled Alice's head in her lap.

"Poor Alice has fainted," she cooed. "Oh, Mr. Allen, I told her you wouldn't let those Mexicans hurt us."

Allen ignored her. When he spoke to Black, his face held a sardonic smile, and an indefinable something in his eyes made hackles of fear run up and down Black's spine.

"I came to tell you I sort o' sense the greasers is framin' somethin', so I figures we better all get set," he said softly.

Desperately Black tried to figure whether or not Allen had overheard their conversation. He bent over his wife and drew her to her feet. Then he half carried her from the room.

"She's plumb scared," he said. "I reckon I better be with her when she comes-to."

Allen stepped aside to let him pass, then, with another strange smile, vanished to take his place at the loophole in the centre room. Slats' face was strained as he turned to Nina.

"Do you reckon he heard?"

The girl shuddered.

"He's a devil — a devil! Even if he didn't hear what we said, he suspects. I feel like his eyes can read your thoughts."

Black dumped his wife in a corner of the living room and glanced out the window. Everything was quiet without. When he saw her move, he seized her shoulders in his big, hairy hands and shook her until she moaned.

"Wake up," he growled. "I got to put fear in you afore I can do anything else."

Again Black shook his wife. Would she never wake up? If her mind grew clear, he was confident he could terrorize her into holding her tongue. He found a bucket of water in the corner and dashed some of this in her face. She stirred and murmured.

Suddenly Black leaped to his feet and faced the outer door. He heard the crunching of feet. Men were running out there. He leaped toward the loop-hole at the side of the door.

Before he reached it, there came a resounding crash and the door sagged inward. Black knew now what had happened. The Mexicans had made a still attack and had concentrated their strength on one side of the building. He had been so absorbed in the problem of keeping his wife from talking that he had allowed them to approach without resistance.

For a second he stood paralyzed. Then, with the idea that he must keep Alice with him at all costs, he sprang across the room, lifted her in his arms, and dashed into the centre room, slamming the door behind him.

From the triumphant yells of the Mexicans, he knew they had entered the room he had just left.

Allen said no word of reproach. But Black knew he must realize how the Mexicans had been able to batter down the outer door. Allen barred the door to the living room, then pointed to various loose planks and bade Black barricade the door more strongly. Without a word, Black obeyed the command.

When he had finished he said defensively: "It don't make no difference. It just gives us less rooms to defend."

Allen glanced from Black to Slats and Nina, who had run into the centre room at the first alarm. Then he shrugged.

"Not any," he said sarcastically. "Only the wall between us and them now is made of wood."

Black paled. It was true; the wall between the living room and the centre room was of heavy planks. These were stout enough to resist bullets — but they would burn.

"They'll burn us out!" cried Slats.

"From the sounds in there, I reckon that's what they're gettin' ready to do," Allen said indifferently.

With fire as his aid, the Tiger of the Border had them at his mercy. Fire would eat through that heavy wooden partition, which was as dry as tinder, within a few minutes.

Three courses were open to them — to surrender with the possibility of being tortured, to die outside with guns in their hands, or to remain in the adobe and be smothered by the smoke.

Black was in such despair that, when Alice rose to her feet and staggered toward Allen, he made no effort to interfere. He felt they could expect no mercy from the Mexican bandits. Death had tapped him on the shoulder; it made no difference what Alice told the little gunman. What matter whether they died by Allen's guns or by the Mexicans'?

All could hear plainly the spurred feet of the Mexicans thumping about in the next room.

"Gringos!" a voice called through the door.

"That's the Tiger," Nina whispered.

"What do you want?" It was Allen who answered.

"The Golden Rose, or I roast you all like the pigs you are," the Tiger replied.

"He means me." Nina answered a question in Allen's eyes.

"No!" Slats said fiercely.

Tears flooded Nina's eyes. She threw out her hands in a little helpless, dramatic gesture.

"Oh, I must go to save you and the others!" she cried pathetically.

"I'll kill you before I see you go back to that damned greaser," Slats snarled.

CHAPTER
NINETEEN

A Snake

Nina had no desire for a heroic death. It would be far better to return to the Tiger than to be roasted.

"I must go back," she said. "I will."

"Your answer — you have but five minutes," the Tiger warned.

"What of the rest of us?" Black called. Hope was returning to him.

"Return the Rose, and the rest go free," the Tiger promised. He added solemnly: "By my mother's soul, I swear it."

"Then we —" Black grew silent before the challenge in Allen's eyes.

"Gents, we three ain't goin' to give that gal up to that coyote," Allen said quietly.

The very softness of his words gave them additional force. Black and Slats realized that while Allen lived there would be no surrender.

"Besides which," Allen continued, "you got to remember that the Tiger's word ain't worth nothin' a-tall."

"Time presses. Only two minutes, and I touch the match to roast you." A snarl had come into the Tiger's voice.

"Black, lift them things away from the door an' do it as if you was liftin' eggs," Allen whispered.

For an instant Black had a thrill of hope. Perhaps Allen had relented and intended to surrender Nina. Then he realized that Allen would not have requested quiet had he had any intention of giving up Nina. Nevertheless, Black hoped that the little gunman had some desperate plan that might still save them. He obeyed the command.

"Rose, my Rose, I will give you everything you ask," the Tiger pleaded. "You will surely die if you do not come now."

"I —" Nina commenced, but Slats cut her words short by clapping his hand over her mouth.

Black now lifted the last loose plank from before the door, then turned and looked at Allen.

"Gents, we got only one chance," Allen explained in a whisper. "When I say the word, I want you to swing open the door. I'm goin' in there and you two follow me."

"You can't do it!" cried Alice Saunders.

"There must be twenty of them in there," Black said stupidly.

"Don't make no difference if they was a thousand," Allen said. "An old professor once told me about a thing called psychology — which means if you do what the other gent ain't expectin', you got this psychology thing workin' for you, an' it's darned strong medicine."

The other four ignored the impatient, rising demands of the Tiger and stared at Allen. Instinctively they knew that his cheerfulness was not assumed. He

176

seemed actually glad of the chance to face the hazard of his desperate scheme, which to him must surely prove fatal.

Alice alone understood what brought the strange light to Allen's eyes. He welcomed this chance, because it might bring him to the end of his long, lonely trail and in a way which he would not be ashamed to take. She forgot her own peril and laid her hand on his arm.

"You poor boy."

Allen understood her sympathy. He flashed her a smile which she was never to forget.

"Shucks, ma'am, don't you worry none. This here psychology is sure strong medicine."

He drew his two guns and examined them.

The Tiger was still growling oaths and threats on the other side of the door. Black could hear the shuffling of many feet. He knew the room was crowded with bandits — and here was this freckle-faced kid grinning at the idea of leading an attack against them.

"You gals go in the back room. You two gents come asmokin' after me. Try to hit the officers," Allen instructed.

"If he hits the Tiger, it —" Slats spoke to Nina, then grew silent.

The joy left Allen's eyes; they grew sardonic as they rested on Slats.

"If I downs the Tiger, it won't make no difference even if they downs me. The rest will quit. Is that what you meant?"

Slats shuffled his spurred boots uneasily and glanced at Nina. Alice turned and addressed her husband.

"You can't let him go in there alone — not after what you intended to do to him. Haven't you two any manhood in you? To let him sacrifice himself for us after what you intended to do to him!"

Realizing that her appeal was in vain, she broke down and began to sob. Instinctively she knew that neither Black nor Slats intended to follow Allen into that room. They were hoping that Allen would be able to kill the Tiger before he himself was killed, but they would not risk their own skins. With the Tiger dead, the assault would be abandoned.

In a daze Alice watched Allen as he backed a few steps from the door. She saw his face change, grow old. She saw the yellow fire of the wolf leap to his eyes.

Then he nodded, and Black swung open the door.

Alice caught one confused glimpse of a room crowded with tall-hatted bandits. Then Allen ran forward and cleared the pile of brush that the Mexicans had heaped against the door. Even as he was in the air, she heard his heavy guns commence their thunder of death.

Then Black slammed the door and barred it again. With the strength of hysteria, Alice flung herself forward, thrust Black aside and struggled to unbolt the door. As she struggled, there came to her the thunderous roars of many guns and the shrill screams of stricken men.

The Tiger of the Border had realized at last that his pleading was in vain. He had just turned to give the order to fire the brush, piled in readiness against

178

the wooden wall, when the door jerked open and something leaped over the brush.

To the startled eyes of the Tiger and the Mexicans, the thing that catapulted itself among them was more like some beast of prey than a man. It seemed to hang in space for an interminable time, and as it hung there, jagged red flames leaped from it.

The double roar of Allen's guns thundered in the small room. Something smashed against the Tiger's shoulder, whirled him about, and sent him spinning through the outer door to crash in the dust outside. Allen landed on his feet, leaped sidewise straight into the centre of the petrified bandits. As he leaped, his guns again roared out their leaden death. After that, everything was confusion. The bandits fired blindly at that leaping figure with the flaring eyes. They fired crazily and killed their friends.

"*Dios*, the Wolf!"

"*Madre de Cristo*, save me!"

The swirling smoke was an impenetrable fog cut by jagged forks of lightning. Men were deafened by the thunderous roars of many guns. A continuous concussion of sound beat against the walls and rebounded against eardrums.

Two seconds after Allen leaped through the door, the room was so thick with smoke that friend could no longer distinguish friend. Still Allen's guns continued their roar of death.

A man screamed in terror: "He is the devil!"

Others took up the cry and fought to reach the door. They jammed the entrance, fought through it, then

179

streamed up the slope toward their horses and away from the dealer of death in the adobe.

It had taken Alice Saunders scarcely ten seconds to wrench open the door, but when she clambered over the brush, the fight was over.

The roar of the guns had stopped. Slowly the smoke rolled out the doorway, and the room cleared. The woman gave one horrified glance, then covered her eyes with her hands and moaned.

Slats and Black swore, and gaped at each other.

Allen sagged weakly against the wall, his arms sagging straight down, the empty guns still smoking in his hands.

On the floor of the room lay nearly a dozen Mexicans sprawling grotesquely. Allen's guns had taken a terrible toll in that crowded space, and the wild firing of the bandits themselves had added to the destruction. Some lay with startled expression on their faces; others moaned and sobbed out curses and prayers.

Allen grinned weakly at the two men in the doorway.

"I tole you old psychology was strong medicine."

"You're hit!" Alice ran forward and supported him.

"Reckon so, but I've been hit worser." He tried to smile again; then, dropping one of his guns, he raised his hand to wipe away the fog that gathered before his eyes.

Slats and Black still stood in the doorway, paralyzed by this miracle. Nina Tower was the first to recover.

"Quick, Slats! Grab him now while his guns are empty!" she cried.

When they gaped at her and made no move, she ran toward Allen and pushed Alice away. For a moment she shrank before what she saw in Allen's eyes. Then, as he stooped to the floor and groped about for a gun, she sprang on him like a cat and clawed him. He was so weakened and dazed by his wounds that he was no match for her furious strength. He sagged down wearily, and his head rested on the back of one of the fallen Mexicans. His eyes were sardonic.

"Figured you was half snake, but I reckon you're all snake."

He sighed and lapsed into unconsciousness.

With that Slats and Black came to life. They leaped toward the still-open door, cleared the room of the groaning bandits by dumping them outside, then slammed the door and barricaded it with the kitchen table. Slats tied Allen's hands and feet securely with thongs of leather.

Alice was too stunned to protest at first. When she did voice her complaint, Black ordered her to shut up and she was forced to still her protests in the face of his brutal threats.

"At least, let me dress his wounds," she pleaded.

"Let the ugly little runt die!" Slats said.

But at last the two men gave grudging consent, and Alice bathed, cleaned, and dressed Allen's wounds. Besides the one in his thigh, which he had received earlier in the day, he had two fresh ones. A bullet had ripped through his left arm, fracturing one of the bones, another had torn its way along his ribs.

181

In spite of the fact that Allen was unconscious and wounded, the men still feared him. They were adamant in their refusal to allow Alice to unbind him the better to dress his wounds. Even when she pointed out that his arm was broken, they refused to allow her to loosen his bonds.

"He stays tied up until I get him in jail at Weston," Slats declared. "Then I'm going to keep him ironed, hand and foot, until I take him out and hang him."

"You cowards! He's sick, and you still fear him!" Alice cried scornfully.

Slats flushed, for he knew she spoke the truth.

"Shut up!" he snarled.

Alice would have said more, but her husband took a threatening step in her direction. She paled and grew still. The memory of the blow he had struck her recently made her tremble.

"Fear him? Nonsense! He's worth twelve thousand dollars!" Nina said gleefully.

The Mexicans made no further attack on the adobe, although they did fire at it occasionally. Neither Slats nor Black knew that the Tiger had been wounded. They could not understand why he held his men back. The truth was that, after the Tiger had been hit by Allen, he had been carried away by one of his men.

CHAPTER
TWENTY

White Wolf's Pack

The sun was a red disc in the west, and long shadows veiled the stark bareness of the valley, when Slats Higgins gave an exultant whoop and threw open the door. Clearly outlined against the sky, he saw the whole band of Mexicans galloping rapidly toward the border.

A short time later, Deputy Sam Stevens and a small posse arrived. The deputy was a short, squat man with a square face and abnormally long arms.

"'Lo, Slats." He gazed about the clearing. "Sort o' looks as if you was having a warm time."

Slats glanced from Black to Nina and back to the deputy. He drew a deep breath as though he braced himself for a plunge, then shook his head. What he had intended to say was too much for him. Nina had no such scruples.

"That's not all — step in here," she said to Stevens, and led the way into the living room.

"Gosh!" Sam Stevens said. "Must 'a' been some fight!"

"It sure was!" Black grinned maliciously at Slats.

"And do you know who led the greasers?" Nina asked, and paused for effect. "The Tiger of the Border! And look!"

Dramatically she flung out a hand and indicated Allen.

"Great gosh, you got the Wolf!"

The deputy and the posse gaped at Allen, who had regained consciousness. He was suffering agony from his broken arm, because of his bonds. His face was pale and haggard, but his strange eyes were pools of sardonic mirth.

"Yes, the Wolf. He was joint leader with the Tiger of the bandits. Slats met him face to face and beat him to the draw," Nina continued, unashamed.

"Beat him to the draw!" The deputy stared from the Wolf to his chief.

"Quit kiddin'!" said another of the posse.

Unwilling, Slats looked at Allen and he flushed at what he saw in the little outlaw's eyes. More than contempt lay there. At that moment Slats hated Allen, hated him as one can only hate a person whom one has wronged. He longed for Allen to deny his story, to brand it a lie — anything that would give him the opportunity to smash that contemptuous face with both of his fists. But Allen said nothing. He continued to look at Slats as one might regard a strange beast, in mingled curiosity and wonder.

Slats turned away. He could face Allen no longer. Roughly he pushed his way through the posse and went outside. Nina cast an appealing glance at Black, who seemed to be struggling with suppressed mirth.

"Tell them, Black. Didn't Slats drop Allen in fair fight?" she demanded.

Black grinned and nodded. Nina's intuition told her that Allen would never deny her story. His pride would forbid it. She turned and pointed her finger at him.

"Didn't Slats down you?" she demanded.

Allen's face did not change. He looked at her with that same wonder and curiosity which he had turned upon Slats.

"See, he doesn't deny it. He doesn't dare."

"Gosh, it don't seem possible, but maybe he did," the deputy said in awe.

Allen was carried back to Weston in a wagon procured from a neighbouring ranch. The trip was torture to him. Several times he fainted from the agony of his bound and broken arm. But never once did he complain, nor by word or sign did he plead to have his bonds loosened.

Toward the end of the trip Alice received permission to ride in the wagon with him. Slats had consented to this, because he wished to have Allen alive when they entered Weston. He wanted to make a triumphal entry.

During this last part of the trip Allen got from Alice her own story. It was a sordid enough little story — a girl's infatuation for a dashing man. After marriage had come disillusionment. She had endured worse than slavery for the sake of her two children.

"What can I do?" she sobbed. "There is no work for me in Weston. I have no money with which to run away. And where could I go? I would not leave without my children."

"Shucks, ma'am, you've sure had a hard time." Allen closed his eyes and gritted his teeth as the wagon jolted over a rut. "No one's blamin' you, ma'am. You had to stick up for your kids. Don't you give up hope. Luck is sure to change."

She looked at him in silence and marvelled that a man so tortured by pain could find time to console another. She understood now more than ever why that light of joy had sprung to his eyes when he was about to enter the room with the Mexicans. For years life had dealt him only poor cards, yet he was too much of a man to quit. To cash in on the game for others was different. He had leaped joyfully into that room, because he had hoped it was to be his last hand.

"I'm so ashamed that anyone connected with me should have betrayed a man like you," Alice sobbed.

"Shucks, now, don't go gettin' yourself all tangled up in loose language."

Alice attempted to loosen his bonds, but Allen refused to let her touch them.

"As long as Black is your husband, you can't do nothin' against him, 'cause if you did, you might be plumb sorry afterward," he explained.

Slats' entry into Weston was a triumphal procession. Nina Tower was as proud of him as though he had really done the things for which the people cheered him. By the time he reached the town he had lost all reticence and shame. He told everybody the story of how Black and himself had beaten off the Mexicans; of how at the end he had downed Allen in a gun fight.

186

People crowded about the wagon when it drew up before the jail. They pushed and shoved for a chance to see the famous outlaw. Allen fought back the pain and even managed to grin. He was anything but a formidable-looking captive. Always thin, he now looked like a sickly schoolboy.

"Gosh, 'tain't possible that there skinny kid is the Wolf?" marvelled one spectator.

"It's sure hard to believe, but I reckon it's so," another replied.

Allen summoned his strength by a last effort of his will and managed to walk into the jail unassisted. But when he reached the cell block, he tumbled to the floor in a dead faint.

When he came to he found himself in a large single cell in the second story of the prison. Handcuffs were on his wrists and irons about his ankles.

"This here is the condemned cell where we brings gents who is due to get their necks stretched," Sam Stevens told him. "You ain't tried proper yet, but the sheriff says it's so darned sure you'll get hanged, he figured you might as well get used to it."

The next morning the Weston *Clarion* carried a glaring front-page headline:

THE WOLF CAUGHT AT LAST!

Below was a glowing account of Allen's capture. Slats Higgins was pictured as a superman, an officer of the law who, with a single companion, had not only defeated the Tiger of the Border and his band of

187

outlaws, but had shot it out with the Killer Wolf and emerged victorious. The story ended with this sentence:

Two weeks from to-day is Election Day. We suggest that, under the circumstances and in respect to valour, the opposing candidates retire gracefully and make the re-election of Slats Higgins for sheriff unanimous.

The story created great excitement in Weston. The opposing candidates retired promptly. Nina Tower plumed herself, took her share of reflected glory, and almost consented to marry Slats before he received the reward.

The story of Allen's capture leaped from county to county, then from State to State. At last the Wolf had come to the end of his trail.

But there were men scattered through every State west of the Mississippi who read that story, pondered over it, and came to the conclusion that the version of Allen's capture was a lie. But that was of no great importance. The important thing was that Jim Allen had been caught and was already virtually condemned before he had been tried. These men packed their bags without further ado and headed toward Weston. They did not know what they could do; their only thought was to be on hand in case something turned up.

Among them were old prospectors, ranchers, and nesters. Three sheriffs started on that pilgrimage and two Texas Rangers. Besides these respectable citizens,

"I hears tell they catched the Wolf. I never see a gent hanged lawful, so I reckon I'm headin' for this here Weston," he told Dandy, with a toothless grin.

"That so? Well, they sure want me bad in that there State, but I'll drift with you." Dandy smiled thoughtfully. "You know they had a rope around my neck when Jim horns in and shows them they has the wrong party."

"The Apaches had me spread-eagled and was startin' to play tunes on my nervous system when Jim rides 'em down with a gun in each hand," Baldy said, with another grin.

"That so? Let's go see him strung up." Dandy smiled thinly.

For two days Slats Higgins exhibited Jim Allen to the curious at two bits a head, as though he was a strange animal. Slats chuckled to himself and rubbed his hands with glee at the endless stream of people who were willing to pay to see the famous outlaw. Black Saunders, Nina, and he were counting the days until they would receive the reward.

On the third day Slats received warning of the coming storm.

Doctor Patterson was a personage in Weston and a difficult man to be put off. He did not tell the sheriff that Jack Allen had retained him by wire; he simply insisted on seeing Allen.

"It's rumoured in town that Jim Allen needs medical attention," the doctor said. "Why not let me see him and put these rumours to rest? If you refuse, I must believe them."

other wolves answered the call of the pack. One of their own was in a trap.

All the men who came to Weston at the news of Allen's capture had one thing in common. Each owed the White Wolf a debt and each was willing to hold his life in his hands to pay.

Jack-twin Allen, in far-off Wyoming, read a garbled account of his brother's capture. He turned in his U.S. marshal's badge, packed his two guns in a bag, and boarded a train to Weston.

Toothpick Jarrick and Snippets MacPherson heard the news in Beaverville. Toothpick protested when Snippets insisted that she was leaving for Weston at once.

"Look here, Snippets, you can't do nothin'. I'm headin' south pronto. You stay here. Your dad will raise merry hell if you pull out."

Snippets' dark eyes flashed; Toothpick squirmed uneasily beneath her regard.

"Toothpick, you know what Jim Allen means to me. Not once, but three times, he saved my life and my father's life. He is caught like a rat in a trap. I'm going to him."

Toothpick shrugged. He knew Snippets. There was no stopping her.

"I'll amble into town and see about trains," he said.

Then there was "Baldy" Small, a wizened old reprobate. The news came to Baldy in El Crucifixio, that outlaw town sprawled across the border. He sough out "Dandy Dan," the gambler.

Slats was forced to accede. What Doctor Patterson said after he saw Allen made the sheriff's ears redden. Patterson set Allen's arm and dressed the wounds, which had become inflamed. He insisted that the handcuffs be taken off until Allen's arm had set. Slats made a quick about-face and ordered the cuffs to be taken off. But the moment the doctor left, he had them replaced.

CHAPTER
TWENTY-ONE

Fasting

On the fifth day, Jack Allen arrived. At first Slats refused to let him see his brother.

"Mr. Higgins, you sure tell a fancy story when you relate how you took Jim. I hear tell you let folks see him at two bits a head. There's two bits. If my money ain't as good as other folks', I'll sure want to know why."

Jack Allen's voice was brittle as ice. Slats moved uncomfortably under the bleak gaze of the whiskered little officer of the law. He was forced to consent.

But he heaved a sigh of relief when Jim Allen refused to speak to his brother. Jim advised Jack in surly tones to go back to Wyoming and mind his own business. Jack Allen shrugged and stalked out without a word.

That afternoon Sam Stevens buttonholed Slats and drew him aside.

"Look here, boss, you noticed a bunch of strangers has hit town?" he asked. "Yesterday a gent could call Jim Allen a parcel of names and nobody here doubted your story. But these here strangers is talkin' loud. It ain't safe to talk about Jim Allen no more. A while ago Sim Brown said over in the Big Bear Saloon that you was a hero and Jim Allen ought to hang, and the words ain't left his lips afore there was three or four hard-faced strangers what called him a liar. And other gents done the same thing to 'Skinny' Moore when he shot off his mouth. Folks is beginnin' to talk. You take my advice and hurry that trial and hang Allen pronto."

Slats took the story to Black and Nina. Both agreed that he had made a mistake in not killing Allen at the adobe. But it was too late for that now.

"Say, I've a good mind to call in the soldiers!" Slats cried.

"A wonderful hero you'd be, if you did that," Nina said contemptuously. "You're supposed to have beaten a coupla hundred bandits with Jim Allen and Tiger at their head, and now you're going to admit you can't keep him in jail."

"Once I get my hands on that reward, I'm goin' to slope," Slats admitted.

"You better stick until you put the rope around the Wolf's neck, because, if he ever gets loose, there's no place in this world where you're safe," Black said grimly.

Slats pulled all the wires he could to get a quick trial.

On the day this farce on justice occurred, the town was crowded. Ten times the number who were able to squeeze into the courtroom were outside in the street when the court opened.

A large collection had been gathered to hire a famous lawyer to conduct Allen's defence. Practically every stranger in town had contributed to the fund. But Allen refused the lawyer's services. He insisted that he intended to make his own defence.

He was tried on the charge of having killed "Boston Pete" in Fargo, a small town on the outskirts of the country, some three years before.

When asked whether he pleaded guilty or not guilty, he shrugged his shoulders and replied: "Boston needed killin'."

After that he refused to say another word. Every one in the courtroom agreed with him that Boston needed killing, but the evidence was clear and the verdict a foregone conclusion. The jury pronounced him guilty.

Allen's expression did not change as he received his sentence from the judge. His was the attitude of complete indifference. He seemed as a man who has been on the rack and can suffer no more.

"The judge is wastin' his words, 'cause that kid is already dead!" a spectator cried, as Allen was led from the room.

Allen's whole aspect and attitude seemed to welcome the verdict, as if he were utterly wearied and longed for sleep.

Each day Alice brought him his dinner and talked to him. In a way he seemed cheerful, for he chatted and laughed with her. He seemed to ignore his fate, or rather to welcome it. Curiously enough, he put on weight.

This cheerfulness worried Slats, Black and Nina. "I tell you them strangers in town is goin' to help him break jail," Black growled. "He ain't scared, 'cause he figures he'll never hang."

Nina tossed her head.

194

"You're wrong. They all hate him and are staying here to see the execution. I've talked to some of them, and men don't lie to me without my knowing it."

"Yeah?" Slats growled. "Well, you're talkin' too much with that there Dandy Dan. You think you're smart, but let me tell you this: maybe them gents is here 'cause they hate him; just the same, I'm goin' to keep both Black and Sam with him constant until I spring the trap two weeks from to-day."

From that time on both Sam Stevens and Black Saunders were Allen's constant companions. They slept in his cell by turn. One of them was always awake.

"You see this, Mr. Allen?" Black held up a double-barrelled sawed-off shotgun. "If them friends of yours tries anything, I aim to empty both barrels into you the minute they starts."

Allen shrugged indifferently. Time after time the two guards attempted to draw him out, to make him talk; but when they spoke to him, he ignored them completely.

The only person to whom he would talk was Alice Saunders. He talked ramblingly to her, telling her of the strange places he had seen, of his many adventures. His very indifference to his fate seemed the saddest part of the affair to Alice.

Baldy and Dandy Dan heard of her constant visits to Allen. They sounded her out, then gave her a note for him which outlined a carefully thought out plan of escape. But when she attempted to pass it to him, he refused to accept it. Later she reported her failure.

"I don't think he wants to be saved," she lamented.

"Well, I've known him a long time and I don't wonder none," said Baldy.

"Just the same, I figure we better stick around," Dandy added.

The next day Nina and Slats were sitting in the sheriff's office, discussing their coming marriage, when two visitors were announced. One was a tall, lanky, tow-headed young man; the other a slender, dark-eyed girl.

"My name's 'Bud' Macklin and this is my sister, Nell," the tow-headed man announced. "We'd sort o' like to see this gent Allen."

"Why?" asked the sheriff.

"Just 'cause."

"Can we see him hung?" the girl asked eagerly.

"Reckon you can, 'cause the hangin' is goin' to be plumb public," Slats stated.

"Wait a minute, Slats." Nina turned to the two visitors. "Are you any relation to Tobias Macklin?"

"He was our dad," the young man replied.

"Let them see him, Slats," Nina said. "This will be fun." At Slats' blank stare she continued: "Don't you remember that case last September?"

Slats gasped.

"Sure! Allen took — Allen killed him!"

"Killed him! He murdered him!" the girl said fiercely.

Slats grinned.

"Sure, come along. I'll show him to you."

He led the way upstairs to the condemned cell.

"There he is, folks," he said, with a flourish.

Allen was talking to Alice while Black and Sam Stevens played cards. He glanced up at the sheriff's words and clipped his sentence off in the middle. For a moment he stared at his visitors, then commenced to grin.

The girl walked forward and gripped the bars.

"You quitter! You quitter!" Her voice was high and impassioned.

"How dare you taunt him when he's helpless?" Alice flared.

The girl ignored her, but her eyes, black pools of light, remained fixed on Allen. His head drooped and he looked at the floor. Seconds slipped by. The girl's eyes were still on Allen. At last he made a gesture with his hand, a weary gesture of resignation.

"Shucks, I'll play the two spots," he said at last.

"You ain't got nothin' else to play," Black jeered.

"You got eleven days," the sheriff reminded him.

Allen seemed to wilt. His cheerfulness dropped away and he cringed.

"Them cuffs hurt me," he whined.

"Them two kids what you made orphans sort o' took the sand out of your craw," sneered the sheriff.

"You murdered him!" the girl cried.

"We're goin' to see him hung," the man reminded her.

"How can you be so cruel to a man who has no hope and no chance?" Alice protested.

"Time for you to go home." Black seized his wife's shoulder roughly and pushed her out of the cell. She went down the corridor, sobbing.

"Look here, sheriff, take those people away," Allen whined. "An' why can't you loosen these cuffs a little? They hurt my arms."

Allen had grown heavier during his confinement. There were puffs of flesh about the steel rings on his wrists. The sheriff glanced at them, then addressed the girl:

"What do you say? Shall I loosen them?"

"No," snapped the man who called himself Bud Macklin.

"There's no use in torturing him," the girl said.

The sheriff grinned and nodded to Black, who loosened the handcuffs slightly.

From that day a change came over Allen. His cheerfulness left him; he grew morbid. Each day Alice visited him and brought baskets of food, supplied by Dandy and Baldy, but Allen refused to eat.

"Sort o' thinkin' of the rope?" Black jeered. "You ain't hungry no more."

Allen threw himself down on the bed and turned his face to the wall.

"You sort o' wilted since I tol' you I'd pepper you with this." Black flourished his sawed-off shotgun.

"I ain't got no chance," Allen whispered.

During the next week he ate practically nothing. Alice Saunders pleaded with him, Black and Sam gibed; but he would not swallow a mouthful.

Alice reported to Baldy and Dandy that it was useless for them to waste their money on more food. Curiously enough, those two did not seem to worry over the news of Allen's fast. They even attempted to persuade Alice to keep away from him and leave him to his fate. But she insisted doggedly that she would visit him until the very last moment.

Each day Bud and Nell Macklin stood outside Allen's cell and hurled insults at him. They did not approach the bars, and their insults grew monotonous, so Black Saunders and Sam Stevens ceased to listen. Slats allowed these daily visits, because they seemed to disturb the prisoner and break his spirit.

Little by little, as the day of the execution approached, Slats' fear of an attempted jail break left him. Allen's dejection was proof that he had no hope. Day by day, the little outlaw grew thinner; by the day before the execution he was no more than a bag of bones.

Slats, his mind at rest, went gaily on with his plans. The reward was to arrive on the morrow. He planned to split it with Black at the same time he married Nina.

Perhaps his contentment would not have been so complete had he had the key to the insult hurled at Allen that day by Bud and Nell Macklin.

"Grey dawn — it'll soon be your last," Nell taunted.

"Behind bars till the end. What do you say, Mr. Wolf?" Bud jeered.

"Barn boy — that's all you are — a yellow barn boy," the girl cried.

"Dark outside. Let's go, sis."

The two departed. Sam Stevens and Black Saunders grinned. The taunts meant nothing to them, but if they had ignored all save the first word in each sentence, they might have understood.

199

"Grey — behind — barn — dark."

Allen interpreted this to mean that his grey horses would be waiting for him at dark behind the jail barn.

"Don't it sort o' get your goat the way me and the sheriff tricked you?" Black asked.

"Aw, hell, why rub it in?" Allen quavered.

"Do you know the sheriff's gettin' married to-night?" asked Sam.

"Yeah, Mrs. Saunders tole me about it," Allen said dully.

"Sort o' funny. You gettin' your neck stretched and him and me livin' pretty on your reward money," said Black.

"I was a fool. You two get the money. Why can't you get my sentence changed to life?" Allen pleaded.

"Nothin' doin'. We don't get the money unless you hang. You know I tried to make Alice tell who was puttin' up for the fine feeds she brings you, but she wouldn't tell. Not that it makes any difference, 'cause me and Sam here sure like the grub you're too scared to eat."

"Come on, have a bite." Sam offered his empty plate. "It don't hurt none to get hung."

"I ain't hungry, but I'd sure like a drink," Allen whined.

"Go on, Black. Go across the street and bring back a pitcher of beer," Sam urged.

"I don't want beer. Bring me some —"

"Something to give you courage?" Black interrupted. He shrugged contemptuously as he looked at Allen's emaciated figure.

"There ain't no use of two watching a poor gimp like you."

He unlocked the door and went out, slamming and locking it behind him. Allen sat hunched in his chair and listened until his footsteps died away. Then he rose to his feet and began to totter back and forth across the room. Because of his leg irons, he could take only short steps. Back and forth, back and forth, he went, as though driven by visions of what awaited him.

Sam Stevens sat in his chair, Black's sawed-off shotgun across his knees. Allen was in irons, weak, broken, and apparently haunted by demons of fear. Soon Sam ceased to watch him. He failed to note that each time Allen turned he came nearer and nearer.

Allen passed him then stopped. His ten days of fasting had not been in vain. He was a scarecrow of a man. The flesh had shrunk from his hands; they were no more than skin and bones. As he reached the corner, he threw each thumb over in turn and slid off the handcuffs. Then, turning like a flash he swung them up and brought them down on Sam Stevens's head.

The deputy slumped in his chair. Allen seized the shotgun with one hand and with the other steadied the stunned man. Gently, carefully, he balanced him in the chair, then jammed the deputy's hat over his face.

CHAPTER
TWENTY-TWO

Eternal Hope

Allen seated himself at the table, with the shotgun hidden beneath it. Soon he heard a heavy tread on the stairs. He almost hoped it would prove to be the sheriff instead of Black Saunders.

"Hey, Sam," boomed Saunders, as he unlocked the cell door, "wake up. That's a hell of a way to keep guard."

He was standing in the door with it unlocked behind him when Allen leaped to his feet. Black found himself staring into the muzzle of his own sawed-off shotgun.

"Sam! Your cuffs!" he stammered.

Allen grinned.

"I starved myself to make my hands thin enough to slip out of them. You remember how you tol' me you wanted to shoot me full of the slugs in this gun?"

Black grew deadly pale. His hypnotized eyes stared into the black muzzles.

"Then see how you like 'em."

With a motion swift as light, Allen threw the gun to his shoulder and pulled both triggers. The last thing that Black Saunders saw on this earth was the double red flare.

Allen cast the gun from him and picked Sam Stevens's .45 from its holster. Then he hurried from the cell to the window at the head of the staircase. Because of the irons on his feet, it was impossible for him to take long steps, but he reached the window and flung it open just as the pounding footsteps below warned him of the jailer's approach.

He slid through the window and dropped to the ground. He was greeted by Toothpick Jarrick, who practically caught him in his arms.

"I heard the shootin' and come a-runnin'," the puncher explained.

"Hello, Mr. Bud Macklin," Allen said. "I reckon we could make better time if you carried me. These irons on my legs make it sort o' hard to run."

Toothpick lifted him, eased him over one shoulder, and ran along the jail wall toward the barn. There he called out to several dark waiting figures.

"Here's the little jailbird."

He planted Allen on his feet and grinned at the men who moved forward through the darkness. Allen braced himself and peered about.

"Where did all you gents come from?" He paused. "Huh, I know this little runt who wears six-inch heels tryin' to make folks think he's a real man."

"You gosh danged —" Jack Allen finished in a flow of lurid chaff.

"Darn you, I tol' you to ride when you first come around," Allen said querulously.

"Did you figure I'd go leave you?" Jack Allen asked quietly.

"What right's a sheriff got helpin' a jailbird break jail?"

Everyone there recognized that Jim Allen was both sorry and pleased that his brother had risked everything to save him. Several of the party listened anxiously to shouts and hurrying feet in the jail that told that the news was being spread of the Wolf's escape.

Snippets MacPherson glided out of the darkness and put a hand on each of the brothers' shoulders.

"You boys behave," she admonished. "We've got to get out of here."

Jack Allen laughed, but Jim was silent.

"Huh, so it's my friend, Nell Macklin?" he said at last. "Now tell me how I can get out of here with these anklets on?"

But Snippets, who had helped arrange the details of the escape, had thought of that. Allen sat on the ground and laid his shackles across a stone. A man armed with cold chisel and hammer started to work on them. A few ringing blows, and the chain parted.

"Get goin', Jim. The whole town is bein' aroused," Jack Allen admonished.

Jim Allen listened for a moment to the shouts in the jail. Then he grinned.

"There ain't no hurry, Jack. You ain't used to this sort of stuff, or you'd know them folks has to holler for half an hour afore they get set to do anything."

The other members of the rescuing party crowded forward. As he recognized them Jim Allen was too overcome to speak for a moment. He knew the distances these men had travelled, the dangers they had risked for his sake.

"'Lo, Baldy, you old hoss-thief. 'Lo, Dandy. An' gosh, if that ain't old 'Flatfoot' an' 'Boston Jack'! Huh, an' if that ain't Bob Tomlinson! Say, Jack, you sure is in bad company. Every other dang man here except you and Toothpick is a no-good outlaw. You want to keep your hand on your watch."

He talked fast to hide his feelings. These were real friends. He said nothing to thank them; words were too small. When he felt Princess, his old grey mare, nose his pockets for sweets, his voice broke. He leaped into the saddle.

Then the group of ten horsemen and the girl rode out of town by a roundabout way.

Slats Higgins was jubilant as he left town that evening and rode toward the Armstrong ranch. The Golden Rose awaited him there. He was to marry her. Armstrong was the political boss of the county and he had insisted on making a ceremony of the presentation of the reward. This was to take place first and be followed by the marriage. The moon was rising out of the desert as Slats reached the ranch.

He swung from his horse before the porch and hurried into the big living room. He found ten or twelve couples gathered there. Slats was a little surprised to find so few people. Practically everyone of prominence in the county had been invited.

Nina beckoned him and whispered:

"Armstrong, the fool, has been asking me questions. He says people are saying that the story we told about Allen's capture is a lie. Those strangers in town are the ones. Someone has told them the true story, and they've spread it about."

"So that's why hardly anyone came to-night!" Slats cried. "I bet it's that Saunders woman."

"I told you to run those men out of town," Nina said sharply.

"Don't be a fool! I'd look pretty trying to run Jack-twin Allen and Bob Tomlinson out of town."

"Yes, that's true. I keep forgetting that you didn't really beat the Wolf to the draw and that it was I who disarmed him." Nina's words were heavy with sarcasm.

"Ah, shut up," Slats replied angrily. The two were silent for a moment; then Nina brightened suddenly and smiled at him.

"Slats, the game is up here. You're finished. Let's take the whole twelve thousand and go north to-night."

"And do Black out of his share?"

"It would teach him to make his wife keep her mouth shut," Nina said viciously.

Slats considered this for a moment. Then he nodded. Nina was right. He was through here. He could tell that from Armstrong's face. That man was a politician and an expert in gauging public opinion. There was no cordiality in his manner as he approached Slats.

"Howdy," he said coldly. "You two ready? Let's get started, then."

He raised his voice and addressed the little crowd of people.

"Gents and ladies, you are here to-night to see a valiant and brave sheriff get his reward for his heroic capture of Jim-twin Allen."

Slats flushed at the tinge of sarcasm in Armstrong's voice. The spectators stirred uneasily and looked wonderingly at each other. What did this mean? Armstrong stopped and brought forth two heavy bags from beneath a desk. They clinked as he dropped them on the table before Slats.

"There's the reward. Some folks call it blood money. Six thousand for our sheriff and six thousand for Black Saunders. That ends my part in the affair. We'll let the minister finish it."

He stepped away and the minister advanced and stood before the couple. Both Slats and Nina were in such a cold fury that they mixed their responses. But at last the minister finished.

"I pronounce you man and wife."

"Three cheers for the sheriff and his bride!" someone called.

There was a feeble cheer broken by a sudden startled movement. A crowd of men came pouring into the room by the open doors and windows.

"Good evening, señors. Let no one touch his gun, for all are covered."

Nina gave one glance, then screamed. Slats Higgins went white. His hand jerked toward his gun, but he thought better of it. Hastily he raised his hands above his head.

"Disarm them, Pedro." The Tiger of the Border advanced into the room. "Have no fear, señors. We mean no harm to you."

The room was covered by the guns of twenty of the Tiger's men. Resistance was useless. The wedding guests made no protest at being disarmed.

"Gentlemen, I have come to get my wife." The Tiger pointed toward Nina.

All turned to stare at her. For once in her life Nina Tower seemed at a loss. Panic filled her eyes, and the panic shifted to fright as she marked the sternness of the Mexican's voice and the grim set of his face.

"When news was sent to me that you, my Golden Rose, were about to marry another man, I would not believe it at first. I came and saw with my own eyes."

"I thought you were dead," Nina muttered.

The Tiger shrugged.

"Perhaps. You will now take your dowry and come with me."

Nina's mind worked rapidly. Things would not be so bad if they took the money with them. She summoned a smile and her eyes were soft and appealing, as she stepped forward to lay one small hand on the Tiger's arm.

"We will go together, my brave one."

"You sure will; but you'll leave that blood money here!"

The voice came from the rear of the room. The Mexicans were as much surprised as the others had been a moment before. They gaped at the tattered little figure that stood in the rear door. Allen still wore about

208

each ankle a part of the broken irons. He had not drawn his guns, but his hands hung loosely near them. His freckled face was split in a smile that was not pleasant to look upon.

"Gents, I'm not alone," he continued easily. "If you look out those back windows, you'll see other men who, I promise you, know how to handle a gun. We have no quarrel with you, but we demand two things."

Slats' face was as white as death as he stared at Allen. Allen's sure and easy nonchalance was terrifying in itself. Slats shivered and looked about helplessly.

The Tiger knew his men outnumbered Allen's, but even so, if it came to a fight, there was no certainty that the victory would be his. He dropped his hands from his pearl-handled guns.

"And those two things, señor?" he asked.

"That money there first."

The Tiger shook his head.

"Refused."

Armstrong and the other unarmed Americans sidled away from between the two groups and hugged the walls.

"Señor, hear my story." Allen walked across the floor to the place where the Mexicans had piled the guns of those they had disarmed. He selected one of these and then crossed to Slats. Without a word he dropped the gun in the sheriff's holster, then backed away.

"Gents, Mr. Slats Higgins, your sheriff, tol' a story about how he took the Wolf," Allen said crisply. "I'm goin' to tell you my side of it now. He tol' you all he beat me to the draw. What he done once he ought to be

209

able to do again. So if what I say ain't the truth, he can go for his gun and drop me as he done afore."

Slats licked his dry lips and glanced about. Allen's grin, the easy contempt in his eyes, drove him into a passion of rage. His hand quivered and shook as it hovered over his gun butt. But he did not draw. He knew that if he touched his gun he would never live to see to-morrow's sunrise.

Slowly, relentlessly, Allen drawled out his story. When he had finished he flipped his left hand toward Slats, who shrank back as if from a blow. The sheriff leaned against the wall and shook with fear and utter shame.

"The Tiger here will tell you folks if I tol' the truth," Allen added. "You can see one thing for sure. Mr. Slats sure tol' a lie when he said he gunned me fair. Take a look at him, gents."

They stared at the quivering, shaking man.

"You mean to tell me that after you saved those folks' lives three times, jumped those Mexicans single-handed, they tied you up when you was wounded?" blurted Armstrong.

The Tiger of the Border answered for Allen.

"Señor, he speaks the truth. He came through that door like a devil. We were surprised. He was death and destruction."

He bowed, sweeping the floor with his gaudy sombrero.

"The Tiger greets the Wolf, señor. The money is yours by right."

Allen nodded and glanced at the circle of spectators.

"I'm askin' you if Slats is a skunk."

"I'll say he is!" Armstrong cried.

"The rest of you don't say nothin', so I reckon you agree."

Allen turned and beckoned Toothpick and Baldy. They hurried through the door and picked up the bags of money. Jack Allen disarmed Slats and pushed him out the door.

"Come, my Golden Rose." The Tiger laid his hand on Nina's arm.

His face told the hate which had taken the place of his infatuation for her. She cried out and tried to pull away, but he held her firmly.

"No, no! You can't allow him to take me," she appealed to the watchers. "I'm a woman."

Jack Allen interrupted sternly.

"You're his wife, and you ain't a woman. You're a snake."

The two armed groups slipped from the room. The Americans, with Slats in their midst, went out the back, while the Mexicans, with Nina, departed by the front. They left the spectators in a stupefied silence.

As Allen and his party climbed the hill to the spot where they had left Snippets with Dandy Dan, Allen glanced back and saw the line of Mexicans outlined clearly in the desert, wending their path south.

"Snippets, I want you to take that money what is packed on that hoss to Alice Saunders," he said. "You tell her it belongs to her, and tell her there ain't no

211

reason for her not to take it, 'cause she didn't have no more to do with my escape than my gettin' caught."

Snippets could see his face clearly in the bright moonlight. He tried to smile at her and failed.

"Jim, when I saw you in jail you'd quit, thrown up the sponge," she said softly.

"Yeah, I reckon I had. I was sort o' tired of things," he muttered.

"You promise you'll keep on playing your two spots?"

"Yeah."

"And you'll keep hoping that we'll climb the hill from that valley of yours and take the ladder to the stars," she added softly.

"That ain't possible, Snippets."

"But you can hope."

"Yeah. So-long." He raised his voice and called: "So-long, Toothpick. So-long, Jack, until the next time."

He sat there on his horse and watched Snippets MacPherson, his brother Jack, and Toothpick ride slowly up the moonlit hill. When they had topped the rise, he turned to the others, then pointed at the trembling sheriff.

"What will we do with him?" he demanded.

"Hang him," Boston Jack said bluntly.

The sheriff screamed at that. Jim Allen looked at him and shook his head. Then he turned and looked in the direction Snippets had gone. He was tired of dealing death.

"He ain't worth a bullet or a piece of rope," he announced at last.

The following morning two cow-punchers found the sheriff securely chained to a post before the courthouse. They read the placard hung about his neck.

SLATS HIGGINS — SHERIFF
Found guilty of being a skunk by his folks.

The sheriff pleaded with the two and begged them to turn him loose, but the true story of the fight in the adobe house and of how he had managed to capture Allen had already reached town, so the two punchers turned a deaf ear to his pleas.

"Huh, I ain't touchin' no skunk," one said scornfully.

"Not any, they smell you up," the other agreed.

All that day the miserable man remained chained to the post. There was always a little, jeering crowd about him. It was toward evening when at last someone took pity on him and knocked off his chains. He left town that night and was never seen or heard of again in that part of the country.